Crazy Jacob

KidWitness Tales

Crazy Jacob
by Jim Ware

Dangerous Dreams
by Jim Ware

Galen and Goliath
by Lee Roddy

Ruled Out
by Randy Southern

Trouble Times Ten
by Dave Lambert

The Worst Wish
by Lissa Halls Johnson

KiDWiTNESS
T·A·L·E·S

Crazy Jacob

JIM WARE

BETHANYHOUSE
MINNEAPOLIS, MINNESOTA

A Focus on the Family book.
Published by Bethany House Publishers
A Ministry of Bethany Fellowship International
11400 Hampshire Avenue South
Bloomington, Minnesota 55438
www.bethanyhouse.com

Printed in the United States of America by
Bethany Press International, Bloomington, Minnesota 55438

Library of Congress Cataloging-in-Publication Data

Ware, Jim

CIP data applied for

ISBN 1–56179–885–1

2 3 4 5 6 7 8 9 10 11 12 13 14 15 / 07 06 05 04 03 02 01

To my wife, Joni.

*And to my kids,
Alison, Megan, Bridget,
Ian, Brittany, and Callum.*

JIM WARE graduated from Fuller Theological Seminary with a degree in biblical studies. He writes for ADVENTURES IN ODYSSEY and Focus on the Family's Radio Theatre.

Andrew lay on his back, gasping for air. Between gasps, he wondered if there could possibly be anyone he despised more than Demas. *Maybe Artemas*, he thought.

Artemas was Demas's uncle. He owned large herds of pigs that grazed on the plateau above the lake. Artemas was a successful, influential businessman. He was as powerful as he was mean-spirited. And Artemas had a bitter grudge against Andrew's father, Jacob.

Demas was nothing but an oversized hulk of a kid who thought being 15 years old made him something special. Andrew would never understand why his father had taken Demas on as an apprentice in the boatbuilding trade. Supposedly it had something to do with a request from Demas's father, who had since died of some disease.

Demas was a big problem. He was big in *every* way— big and beefy and stupid. Artemas liked to say Demas was "large-boned." Demas was cowardly, superstitious, and thick-headed. Worst of all, Demas was, at that very moment, sitting on Andrew's chest, shoving his tousled brown head into the sand on the shore of Lake Kinneret.

"If my father were here . . ." gasped Andrew.

"Whatcha gonna do when he comes, *Jew boy?*" sneered the curly-headed, pudgy-cheeked bully. "Tattle?"

"No, but . . ."

"Guess you know what's good for you!" The larger boy released his victim and stood up. "Now go get me those smoothing blocks!"

Andrew jumped up, brushed the sand from his home-spun tunic, and wiped an angry tear from his freckled cheek. Then he stumbled up the beach toward the shed where his father and Stephen kept their tools.

Working with Demas was no fun. They were sup-posed to be smoothing the hull of a new trading boat. So far, at least half their morning had been taken up with bullying and fighting instead. Jacob wanted the new boat in the water by the next day, early enough to allow time for the planking to swell before beginning to caulk, when they would fill the cracks with pitch. Now they were be-hind schedule. *We'd have been finished by now if it weren't for him*, grumped Andrew.

Stepping in under the shed's leather awning, he picked up two limestone smoothing blocks from the workbench. As he did so, his eye fell on a number of other tools that lay on the bench or hung on hooks along the walls. The big, two-handled saws. The adz and the plane. The bow drill, the hammers, the wooden mallets. Andrew smiled. *One of these days,* he thought, *I'll use these tools to build my own boat. And when I do, I'll sail it as far away from Demas as I can, maybe even clear across the lake to Magdala or Capernaum!*

That was when he heard voices just outside the back wall of the shed. His father's and someone else's—a whiny, nasal voice. The voice of Artemas.

"As for the boy," the voice was saying, "I can put him to work herding my pigs. Why he was ever apprenticed to a boatbuilder, especially a Jewish boatbuilder, is beyond me. It was my brother's decision, not mine."

Andrew's heart leaped. Demas leaving to herd pigs? It was too good to be true! He bent beside the wall to listen more closely.

"I'm sorry, Artemas," he heard his father say. "I have no intention of closing up shop. And as long as Stephen and I are in business, we're going to *need* an apprentice. There's too much work for the two of us."

Closing up shop?

"But Jacob," intoned the voice, "wouldn't you be more comfortable back among your own kind?"

Not this again, thought Andrew. Artemas resented Jacob's Jewishness, as Andrew knew only too well. It was a subject that had caused him a great deal of personal suffering.

"I'm sure they can use a good boatwright over on the Jewish side of the lake," continued the pig man.

"What exactly are you trying to say, Artemas?" Andrew could hear the rising anger in his father's voice.

"Don't you see? A Jew conducting business on our side of the lake—it sends the wrong message. It tends to . . . well, attract other Jews. And once there's a sizable Jewish community, complete with its strange Jewish God and Jewish codes and Jewish dietary laws—no pigs, no pork, and so on and so forth, you understand—it puts a businessman like myself in a rather awkward position."

I'd love to see you in an awkward position, thought Andrew. *Like on your back in the sand, with a big pig sitting on your head!*

"Artemas," said Jacob quietly, "I am a craftsman. I did not come here to teach anyone about the Jewish God. I fear *all* the gods—Jewish or otherwise! And I have no interest in enforcing Jewish dietary laws. That is *not* why I came to Gadara!"

There was a pause. Then Artemas cooed, "Perhaps a little gift will help you see things my way." Andrew heard the clink of coins in a bag. "I beg you to reconsider."

"Good day to you, Artemas!"

There came a sound of coins scattering in the sand, then a muffled curse and heavy footsteps retreating up the beach. In the next moment Jacob poked his head inside the shed. "Andrew!" he said, looking surprised.

"Have you . . . been here long?"

"Um, no, not really, Father." Andrew blushed. "I only came in to pick up these smoothing blocks."

"Hey! Where are those—?" blurted Demas, jogging up at just that moment. He stopped short when he saw Jacob standing beside his son. "Oh. Good morning, Master Jacob," he finished. "I was just looking for young Andrew here. We have a lot of work to get done."

"You do indeed," said Jacob, rubbing his bearded chin and frowning thoughtfully. "The merchant expects that boat by the end of the week."

"Just what I was telling young Andrew!" said Demas. He grabbed the smoothing blocks and headed back toward the unfinished hull.

A knowing look passed between father and son as the older boy hurried away. "Don't worry," said Jacob, wrinkling his brow and placing a work-worn hand on Andrew's shoulder. "Everything's under control. We'll show them—all of them—" (at this he touched a leather pouch that hung from his belt) "with the help of the gods and spirits."

Demas!" Andrew heard his father yell. "Strike that sail! *Now!*"

It was late the following afternoon. Andrew, Demas, Jacob, and Stephen were out on the lake in the freshly smoothed but uncaulked boat. A stiff wind had just begun to blow.

Crouching in the bow of the vessel, his nostrils filled with the scent of cedar planks, Andrew looked north to where a bank of dark clouds, edged with red, hung menacingly over the water. The wind gusted and flipped a strand of brown hair over his eyes. Two big raindrops slapped him on the cheek. He knew what it meant— another one of Lake Kinneret's unpredictable late afternoon storms.

The iron ring at the top of the mast rattled as Demas hauled on the sheet rope to furl the sail and lower the yard to the deck.

Stephen, Jacob's smooth-shaven Greek partner, was

already handing out oars. "Can you row?" he asked with a playful wink.

"Didn't I learn from the best?" retorted Andrew, grabbing an oar.

He could row, all right. He was proud of his growing abilities as boatbuilder and sailor at only 11 years old. He'd been working with Demas and Stephen and his father for over a year. And he was excited about having a chance to test his skills against the elements. *It'll be fun*, he thought.

"Scared?" prodded Demas as he sat down heavily beside Andrew on the rowing bench. "You can tell *me.*"

Andrew scowled back.

"Get ready!" Stephen shouted into the rising wind. He pulled his linen tunic over his head. "By all the gods! Boreas must be angry! This came out of nowhere! Can you bring her about, Jacob?"

"I think so," answered Andrew's father, leaning hard on the steering oar. "As long as you three can get her moving!"

A feeling of pride swelled in Andrew's chest as he looked back and saw his father standing at the tiller. *What is there to be scared of?* he thought, carefully fitting his oar into the lock. *Father's at the helm.*

Jacob peered north from under brows as dark as the sky itself. The wind ruffled his gray-streaked hair and beard. There was a look of concern on his sunburned face. But Andrew wasn't worried. *Father's the best navigator on the whole lake,* he thought.

"By Meonen, Andrew!" said the helmsman, catching his son's stare. "This is a piece of bad luck! You'll have to row like a man if we're to get her beached before the whole sky breaks loose. There're only four of us, and we built her for a crew of 12!"

"You heard him," hissed Demas, digging an elbow into Andrew's ribs and whispering into his ear. "Like a *man,* not a shrimp Jew boy."

Andrew gritted his teeth. Why couldn't Demas just leave him alone? *Always* there was Demas, and *always* Demas was picking on him. What made it worse was that most of the kids in Gadara had started following his example. They all called him "Jew boy" now. It was so bad that Andrew had stopped going to the academy in town.

Andrew sighed. Why didn't his father just let Demas go to work for his uncle herding pigs? He wished he could punch Demas's fat, mocking face. Instead, he pulled on his oar with all his might.

They all did. In response, the boat turned in the water and jumped lightly toward the shore. Andrew felt a thrill of delight as the hull rose and fell. He couldn't help thinking of the design they'd used in building her; she really *was* a *dancing ship.*

He remembered the care with which his father had

laid her keel, how painstakingly he had smoothed and shaped her high-curving ends with the adz and plane. He recalled with satisfaction how precisely the cedar planks of the shell—the *homoth*, or "walls"—had been fitted together with mortise and tenon and dowel. And he smiled as he pictured the stern patience in his father's face whenever he had to correct Andrew for fudging on the spacing between the joints.

Andrew had refitted some of those joints four or five times; in the end, not one of them was more than a finger's width distant from the next. It was a lot of hard and very tedious work. But when the result was an approving nod from his father—and a hull as snug and tight as the finest cabinetry—Andrew knew it was all worthwhile. No boat on the lake was better made or more seaworthy.

A sudden downpour jarred him out of these pleasant thoughts. A blast of wind shoved the boat sharply aside and threw him against his rowing partner.

"Put your backs into it!" shouted Jacob. "And call upon the gods and spirits of the winds!"

Andrew turned and searched his father's face, but he saw no clue as to his father's feelings. Jacob might have been a stern-faced god himself, standing there between sky and sea with his hand on the tiller. *No need to worry. We'll be back on shore in no time at all.*

"Your father's an odd one, Andrew," laughed Stephen, leaning over backward with the force of his rowing. "A Jew calling upon the gods and spirits! Ha!"

"Sailors need all the help they can get," shouted the steersman, overhearing his partner's comment. "And they don't care where they get it!"

The waves were higher and wilder now. Andrew strained against his oar. Sweat and rainwater dripped from his hair into his eyes. The wind grew colder and beat him about the head until his ears began to hurt.

"Are we getting anywhere, Stephen?" he grunted between strokes. "I can't see a thing!"

"Leave the seeing to your father!" shouted his dark-haired friend. "You keep rowing!"

The sinews and tendons in Stephen's wiry arms stood out in bold relief as he plied his oar. He was a small man, not much bigger than Andrew himself, but very strong. Aside from his father, Stephen was the man Andrew admired most.

Already two or three inches of water had collected in the bottom of the boat. If this kept up, they'd have to stop rowing and start bailing. And the rain was increasing.

This is hard work! thought Andrew. He turned his face upward and stuck out his tongue, drinking in the rain to ease the dryness in his mouth and throat. A strange feeling was growing in the pit of his stomach. His heart pounded rapidly. This wasn't turning out to be as much fun as he'd expected.

He stole a sidewise glance at Demas. The older boy's heavy face had grown pale and his thick, red lower lip was beginning to tremble.

"Aeolus! Zeus! Baal Obh!" cried Demas, dropping his oar and thrusting his thick arms skyward. "Save us and I'll kill you a fat pig!"

A fat pig is right! thought Andrew. But he said nothing and went on rowing even harder than before.

"Yahweh!" shouted Jacob, turning his face up to the clouds. "May Yahweh, God of storms, and lucky Meonen help us now!"

He's calling on Yahweh. Andrew knew that, for all his father's interest in spirits and the unseen world, he rarely prayed to the God of his own people. He wondered why he was praying to Him now.

Suddenly the boat lurched and tilted. A sheet of spray flew over their heads as the high, pointed prow crashed through an oncoming wave. A loud cry came from the stern. Andrew turned to see his father lose his grip on the steering oar and fall heavily against the bulwarks. The boat tipped and shuddered.

"Quick!" shouted Stephen, grabbing Andrew by the shoulders and shoving him toward the rear of the boat. "Take the tiller and hold her steady or we're going to end up with a man overboard! Row hard, Demas!"

Dazed, Andrew grabbed the steering oar and leaned on it. Stephen jumped into the stern, seized Jacob by the wrist, and pulled him to his feet. Andrew's father gave his friend a grateful look.

"It's all right," said Jacob, placing a hand on Andrew's shoulder and resuming his post. "Back to your rowing! We won't get a single drachma for this boat if she ends up at the bottom of the lake!"

At the bottom of the lake! Shaken, Andrew slid back into his place beside Demas and rowed feverishly. This time he dared not look the other boy in the face. But at odd moments, through the roar of the storm, he thought he heard muffled sobs coming from the other end of the bench.

Doggedly, they fought their way through the rising waves and shifting winds. Soon Andrew was conscious of nothing but the rhythm of his body—pull, lift, push, dip; pull, lift, push, dip—over and over again, minute after everlasting minute. He rowed until his mind was as numb as the muscles in his arms.

When at last the boat's keel ground against the pebbles on the shore, Andrew was almost too tired to care. He wanted to slump down into the sloshing water in the bottom of the boat and never get up again.

"Everyone out!" he heard his father shout. Stephen and Demas leaped ashore. Reluctantly, Andrew followed, heaving himself over the side. Then they all laid hold of the boat and dragged her up the beach.

"Andrew!" came a woman's voice from across the sand. "Where's Andrew?"

"Here, Mother!" They dropped the boat on the sand and Andrew ran to meet her. For a long moment, he stood hugging her silently.

Jacob joined them. "It's all right, Helena," he said.

"We made it!" said Andrew. "Didn't we, Father?"

"Yes," agreed Jacob, glancing back at the following darkness. "With the help of the powers."

For a moment, Helena eyed her husband intently. Then she took his arm.

"Do you have any idea how you frightened me?" she asked as the little group hurried up the beach through the wind and the rain. "I never *dreamed* you'd be on the water in such weather!"

"You worry too much," Jacob teased, pushing a dark ringlet aside and kissing her on the forehead. "We finished the planking this afternoon. I thought we had time to tighten the seams, that's all. It has to be done before caulking. You know how quickly these afternoon storms come up. At any rate, we made it back—thank the gods."

" 'Thank the gods' is right!" chimed in Stephen, giving Andrew a hearty slap on the back. "We've seen a little bit of *their* power today, haven't we, boy?"

"I guess so," responded Andrew.

"You *guess* so!" snorted Demas. "Huh! I s'pose *you* believe in that phony Jew god! Right?"

"That's enough, Demas!" shouted Jacob, turning severely on his apprentice. "Now stow these oars and go on home!"

"Yes, sir," answered Demas, meekly lumbering off to the shed.

"I'm just glad you're all safe!" said Helena, releasing Jacob's arm. "I'd better hurry home and finish our supper. Lyra's there by herself."

"The boy and I will be along just as soon as everything's secured here," said her husband, eyeing the sky. "I don't think we've seen the worst of this yet."

Andrew saw his father take his mother's hand and squeeze it hard before letting her go.

CHAPTER 3

So—tomorrow," said Stephen, as Andrew helped him lash down the last of the leather tarps. With the shed covered, their tools would be protected against the wind and weather.

"Early," said Jacob. "We've got at least a couple of days' work left."

"Right," agreed Stephen, gathering his short cloak about him. "Good night, then!" he shouted as he hurried away. "And be careful up there. It's no place to get caught on an evening like this!"

Then Andrew followed his father to the grounded boat. Working quickly, they drove four long, wooden stakes into the sand and lashed the boat to them with strong ropes—a precaution against the wind. After that, they threw another tarp over the boat and tied it down securely.

"All right—let's go!" shouted Jacob. "We'll take the shortcut!"

The shortcut! Andrew shot his father an anxious

glance. Then he followed him through the rain to a spot where a tan-colored dirt path snaked its way out from between gray rock walls. From here it was a short but steep climb to the top of the cliff—a natural palisade rising rapidly to a height of about two hundred feet above the shore of the lake.

Normally, Andrew knew, his father would have avoided this path. But today they were in a hurry. There were other roads home, but this was the quickest and most direct. On the negative side, it was difficult and narrow. And there was another point worth bearing in mind: It went past the Haunts of the Dead.

Andrew knew how his father felt about spirits. Like most sailors, Jacob was as cautious as he was resourceful. His interest in the supernatural world had always been strong, but recently it had grown into an obsession. For some reason, Andrew sensed, his father was more anxious than ever to keep the "powers" on his side. Failing that, he'd do everything he could to protect himself from them.

"Father," said Andrew, looking up at him with troubled eyes, "do you think it's . . . safe?"

In answer, Jacob stopped and untied a leather pouch that hung from his belt by a scarlet cord.

"An amulet," he explained. "It contains *baaras*— 'burning root'—an herb my forefathers considered very powerful. They say that Solomon, the greatest of our kings, used it to ward off demons and evil spirits."

With that, Jacob turned and trudged up the slippery path. Andrew pulled his cloak over his head and hurried after his father.

"Was Solomon afraid of spirits?" he asked when they reached the trail's first sharp turn.

"I don't know," puffed his father. "What counts is that he knew how to *control* them. He feared Yahweh, the God of Israel, too. It's no wonder they called him the wisest of men."

It was growing dark. The wind gusted this way and that among the rocky clefts, pelting them with rain as they labored upward. Every so often the path took them past black, gaping holes in the rock.

Andrew looked away as he hurried past one of these caves. Had he really seen something moving in its murky depths? Why did he have such a strong feeling that the darkness within was full of eyes? A choking lump was rising in his throat. He tried hard to think about the hot dinner waiting for them at home.

Suddenly there came a strong blast of wind. Andrew dropped to his hands and knees to avoid being swept off the face of the cliff. He saw Jacob pointing into the dark recesses of one of the caves. "In here!" his father shouted above the wind's roar. "It's becoming too dangerous to go on. We'll just have to take shelter and wait it out!"

In there? thought Andrew. *I don't believe this!* But it

was either the cave with his father or the bare cliff with the wind and rain. He hesitated a moment, then followed Jacob into the hole in the rock.

Inside, they crouched together in the dim light, looking out over the troubled face of Lake Kinneret, careful to keep their backs to the shadowy inner spaces of the cavern. Andrew shivered and drew his wet cloak closer.

Glancing up at the black ceiling and the dripping walls, he noticed that their rough surfaces bore the marks of iron cutting tools—marks that were yet another reminder of the very thing he was trying so hard to forget. He did not want to remember that these were not natural caves. That they had been hewn out of the rock by human hands. Dug into the cliffside for a specific purpose.

To house the remains of the dead.

Andrew wished they could talk about something. He wanted to hear Jacob's voice filling the empty cavern. But Jacob was strangely silent. He sat hunched up, cradling the little leather bag in his hands.

Once again Andrew had a strong sense that the darkness behind him was filled with watching eyes—pale, dead eyes. And what was that odd smell? He turned his head ever so slightly. Were those really human shapes standing against the wall at the back of the cavern? Or were they something even worse: ossuaries and sarcophagi, stone boxes and jars filled with bones and rotting flesh?

"Mother's going to be worried," he blurted out at last. "Do you think we'll make it home in time for dinner?"

"Of course." His father's voice was flat and expressionless. As he spoke, he never stopped fingering the leather bag.

Andrew shivered again. *Maybe it would be a good idea to change the subject.* "Father," he said, "I want to build a boat of my own."

Jacob looked vacantly at his son. "Do you?" he said. He seemed to be struggling to bring himself back from some distant place.

"Yes. A *dancing ship*. Like the big one we just finished. Sharp-keeled, wide at the top, with a high, pointed stem and stern. Just big enough for the two of us."

"That's fine," said Jacob. A light was growing in his eyes. *Good*, thought Andrew. He knew how much his father loved to talk boats.

"You know," Jacob went on, moving closer to his son and laying the leather pouch on the floor, "the merchants have promised me another load of good cedar the next time they come through. I'll let you have first pick of the lot." A hint of a smile flickered across his features. "It will be good to work together."

Yes, thought Andrew, suddenly glowing with love

and admiration for his father. It was heartening just to hear Jacob talk about familiar things like cedar planks in this strange and terrible place. The man was his hero, his best friend. Not many Jews living in Gentile territory commanded such universal respect. The Gadarene Greeks knew Jacob as the best craftsman in the Ten Cities. And Andrew was Jacob's son. So what if Demas and the boys from the academy called him "Jew boy" and "half Jew"? He didn't care. He didn't need them. Not as long as he had his father. It *would* be good to build a boat together.

"And Father," Andrew added after a few more minutes of rain and silence, "do you think—when it's finished—I might be able to sail it on the lake *by myself?*"

A change came over Jacob's face. He picked up the bag of *baaras* and squeezed it hard. "Alone?" he said, the emptiness returning to his eyes. "No. Absolutely not. Not without Stephen or Demas or me."

"But Father," Andrew protested, "I've learned so much! I can raise and lower the yard by myself. I know how to tack into the wind and—"

"No!" shouted Jacob with sudden violence.

The cavern grew dim. There was movement in the stale air above their heads. Or so it seemed to Andrew.

"No!" his father yelled again. He jumped up, nervously fingering the leather pouch. "Haven't I told you no a *thousand* times?"

At that instant it was as if the darkness and violence of the storm outside had somehow forced its way into that dank, narrow space. Suddenly the world beyond the cave door vanished. Wind and rain were a distant memory. Watching eyes and rotting bones were forgotten. For Andrew, nothing existed but his father's face. A face distorted with pain and fear. The face of a stranger.

"Father, I—" he spluttered, climbing awkwardly to his feet. He was frightened and confused. Never before— not once—had he so much as mentioned the subject of sailing on the lake by himself.

"*Over* and *over* and *over!*" Jacob spat the words fiercely through clenched teeth. The fingers of his left hand twisted in his beard. His eyes roved over the rock walls of the cave.

"What's the matter, Father?" cried Andrew, stumbling backward as Jacob began to swing the little leather pouch in circles above his head.

"*Chashmagoz!*" Jacob chanted menacingly. "*Merigoz! Bar-Tema!* Haven't I told you *never?* Never *again! Chaliylah lecha meyasoth . . . !*"

Andrew continued backing away as his father's speech became a wild, nonsensical babbling. He stopped only when his shoulder touched the wall of the cave. Never in his life had he felt so afraid.

"Do not tempt me!" Jacob shouted, his face twisted

in anguish. "It would be better—" he stuttered. "It would be better if—"

Andrew flattened himself against the wall as his father's left hand jerked upward. *He's going to hit me!* he thought. He raised an arm to shield his face. Then he slumped to the floor.

Nothing.

In a few moments the silence was broken by the sound of soft weeping. He opened his eyes. From over the hills a spark of the setting sun winked in through the door of the cave. The clouds had lifted. The wind and the rain had stopped. His father was kneeling on the floor, his head in his hands, whimpering like a little child.

"Father," said Andrew, getting up and laying a shaky hand on Jacob's shoulder. "Let's go home. Mother will have supper waiting."

CHAPTER 4

Early morning. The still time between darkness and dawn.

Ssshh-k! Ssshh-k! Sssh-k!

Andrew was planing boards at the workbench under the boat shed's leather awning, intent on his work, unaware of the sounds of the waking world.

Why doesn't Father come? he thought.

Oooooeeeeeoooooo . . .

"Andrew!" said Lyra, running up breathlessly. She dropped to her knees in front of him, spraying the workbench with sand. "What's that weird noise?"

Over their heads, pale rosy fingers stretched across the Galilean sky, changing it gradually from empty gray to clear summer blue. But out on the lake there was mist—wispy, white, swirling mist that hid the bright surface of the water and muffled the sounds of the fishermen coming in from a long night with their nets. And through the mist there came a cry—a single note, long, low, and mournful.

Ooooooooeeee . . .

"There! Didn't you hear it?" she demanded, sticking out her chin and pushing the dark hair out of her eyes.

"It's just a bird, Lyra," said Andrew, keeping his eyes glued to the workbench and the piece of cedar in the vise. "A bittern or a heron. Hunting for fish. You've seen them lots of times."

Lyra stood up, leaned her elbows on the workbench, and rested her chin in her hands. "Whatcha doin'?" she asked, looking up at him out of her big, brown eyes.

"Working on my boat," he answered, trying to sound as annoyed as possible. "Father said he'd come and help me if I got here early enough. Can't you see I'm trying to concentrate?"

The strokes of the plane had to be kept smooth, straight, and even. Otherwise, he'd end up with bumps and dips in the edges of his planks—gaps to fill when it came time to piece them together into a shell.

"Well, anyway, I think that bird noise is *weird*," said Lyra carelessly, jumping up and brushing the sand from her linen shift. "It makes me think of scary creatures . . . monsters in the mist . . . like the ghosts in Father's stories. Don't you think so?"

"No, I don't." Andrew winced at the thought of his father's stories. He didn't like them. Neither did his mother. And Father had been telling them more often lately. Ever since that evening in the cave . . .

"Where is Father, anyway?" he added, glancing up.

The sun had risen, touching the tops of the palms with gold and sending the mist scattering. "Stephen and Demas will be here soon. Then we'll have to start the regular work."

"Father?" chirped Lyra, skipping to the corner of the shed. "Oh, I don't know! He doesn't like to work anymore. He likes to tell stories. Andrew, when do we eat?"

"Eat! How can a skinny five-year-old girl eat so much?" he scolded. "We just had breakfast!"

"But I'm bored!" she whined.

"Well, go hunt for rocks or something," he urged. "I'm busy."

How am I supposed to build a boat and baby-sit at the same time? he wondered. Immediately he felt sorry for even thinking it. Andrew understood the situation all too well. He *had* to keep an eye on Lyra because Mother *had* to go to Gadara to sell her skeins of yarn and bolts of cloth. And mother *had* to sell her cloth in Gadara because things had been "tight" lately—ever since Father began behaving so strangely.

Where is Father? I wish he'd come! He remembered the way he had pictured this project in his daydreams: just the two of them, working together early in the morning, before Lyra or the sun or anyone else got up. It was going to be so great! And it *would* have been great, if only . . .

But no! He wasn't giving up yet! Yes, Jacob *had* been acting strangely. But this project was just the thing to cure him of it. Andrew tried hard to pump up a sense of confidence. His father *would* come. Everything would be the way it used to be. They'd work and talk and talk and work, and then—

"*Chaire!* Good morning!" came a voice like a silver trumpet. "A true craftsman at his work!"

"Oh, hi, Stephen." Andrew grinned as the dark-eyed Greek ducked in under the awning.

"Looking *very* good!" Stephen commented, thoughtfully inspecting the wood in the vise. "You have a fine feeling for this sort of thing—like your father. It's going to be an excellent boat when it's finished."

"I hope you're right," Andrew answered doubtfully. "Father promised to help me, but—"

"I know," Stephen interrupted with a frown.

"I guess everybody knows," sighed Andrew, turning back to his work. *Ssshh-k!* A fragrant curl of cedar dropped to the ground as he drew the plane swiftly down the length of the board.

"Don't worry," said Stephen, touching his shoulder. "Perhaps I can help you myself . . . in a few days . . . once we get on top of things . . ."

"Stephen, what's going to happen? To the business, I mean. Mother says the customers aren't happy."

"Nor the creditors!" agreed Stephen, laying his bread

bag on the bench and picking up a brush and bucket of pitch. "Would you be happy with a man who doesn't finish his work or pay his bills on time?"

"But it's so unlike Father! What are we going to do?"

"I'm not sure. Demas is learning, but he has a *long* way to go. His attitude leaves a lot to be desired. *You* show great promise, but you're just a beginner. If Jacob doesn't snap out of it soon—"

"Andrew!" came a small voice from down the beach. "Look at me! Look at *me!* I'm a heron! *Ooooeeeeoooooo!*"

He looked up. Through the dissolving mist he saw Lyra dancing up and down on one leg atop a big rock that stuck out of the water about 10 cubits from the shore. She was dripping wet from head to toe. Her hands were tucked up under her armpits and her elbows were out at the sides of her body, flapping like the wings of a bird.

Stephen burst out laughing.

"I'd better go and get her," said Andrew wearily. "She swims like a catfish, but I don't think I should leave her out there all by herself."

He dropped the plane and ran down toward the water.

"Stay put, Lyra!" he shouted. "I don't want you to— *unnhh!*"

Before he knew what had hit him, Andrew was lying

on his side with a mouthful of sand. Another runner—someone much bigger and heavier—had slammed into him from the side and sent him sprawling. It was his father.

"*Aaiiiieeeee!*" screamed Jacob, tearing off his outer cloak. His arms flailed this way and that. His hair and beard stuck out wildly around his head. Andrew sat up and gaped. A group of fishermen on the shore dropped their nets and stared.

Now what? thought Andrew. He watched helplessly as his father thrashed his way to the frightened Lyra, yanked her down from her rock, and waded with her back to shore. "Away! Away!" Andrew heard him yelling. "*Away* from here!"

Andrew got to his feet and rushed to meet them. He reached the water's edge just as Jacob, with a frenzied look in his eyes, set Lyra down upon the sand. Wordlessly, the little girl looked up at her brother, brown eyes wide with terror.

Not again! thought Andrew, inwardly groaning. It was the cave all over again! Not that there hadn't been some strange and scary incidents since that night. Andrew and his mother had been disturbed by Jacob's prolonged silences, vacant stares, and unpredictable wanderings. But in all those weeks there had been nothing quite like *this*.

Stephen ran up and joined them. He and Andrew exchanged looks.

"It's all right, Father," Andrew began. "I was just—"

Jacob grabbed him by the tunic. "You should have been watching!" he breathed heavily. *"Watching!"* His eyes burned strangely. Andrew felt as if they were staring right through his body, boring a hole into the cliffs beyond the beach. "I told them—I told *you!*—" he shouted, gazing up at the sky, "to leave her alone!"

Andrew shot a glance at Lyra. Tears trembled on her dark lashes.

Then, just as suddenly as he had seized him, Jacob released his son. He sighed, closed his eyes, and dropped heavily on the sand. Taking Lyra by the hand, Andrew backed slowly away.

"Well, then," Stephen ventured after a tense pause. "It's—ah—good to see you, Jacob."

When Jacob responded, it was in his normal voice. He appeared quiet and calm, though completely exhausted. "Stephen," he said, "have we paid the merchant Hadad-Ezer for that load of cedar and oak?"

Andrew saw Stephen's eyebrows arch upward. "No," the Greek answered. "We can't pay until we're paid. And we won't be paid until we finish Alexander's boat. Are you planning on coming to work today?"

Encouraged by Stephen's straightforwardness and the sudden change in his father's behavior, Andrew spoke up.

"We need you, Father," he said eagerly. "I'll help too. We can do it together! And when we're finished, there's the shell of my own boat to get started on. I've begun the planing, but without you, I—"

Jacob's eyes stopped him in midsentence. They had suddenly become dreadful again—distant and burning.

"W-what is it, Father?" stuttered Andrew. Lyra ran and crouched behind her brother, burying her face in his cloak.

Jacob got unsteadily to his feet and began combing his fingers through his hair. "To work," he mumbled. "Coming to work . . . Hmm . . ." He sounded like a man trying desperately to remember something. "No. Not *there* . . ." He began stumbling up the beach in the direction of the cliffs.

"But Jacob," said Stephen, following his partner and laying a hand on his shoulder, "what shall I tell Hadad-Ezer and Alexander?"

"To the tombs," muttered Jacob, turning and leaning into his friend's face. "Tell them I'm going to the tombs."

As Andrew watched, the confusion in his father's eyes gave way once more to angry fire. Suddenly Jacob wrenched Stephen's hand from his shoulder. "Yes!" he shouted. "Tell them I've gone to the Haunts of the Dead! I'm wanted there!" With that he ran off.

Just then Demas arrived for work. "Family problems?" said Demas with a significant sneer. "*I* understand. Uncle Artemas has told me *all* about it."

"You're late, Demas," said Stephen, shrugging his shoulders and walking back toward the boat shed.

Lyra whimpered softly. Andrew sat down on the sand and put his head between his knees.

CHAPTER 5

The clay weights that hung from the bottom of the loom clacked noisily. Even out in the road Andrew could hear them. He stopped to listen as he approached the courtyard. It was a sound he had known all his life, and it never failed to bring him a measure of comfort—something he needed badly right now. Shoving old Baal, the stubborn gray goat, out of his path, he pushed the gate open and stepped wearily into the enclosure.

"I'm home, Mother," he called, mopping his forehead with his old felt cap and sitting down on a wicker crate.

Helena wiped her eyes with the corner of her robe as she turned from her weaving to greet him. "The sun—" she explained.

"I know, Mother," he agreed, doubtful that any amount of glare could cause so much redness in her eyes.

Andrew had always loved this part of a summer day. Many, many times in the past—when Jacob was still himself and still living with them—he had savored these peaceful moments in the late afternoon. After long hours of labor at the boat shed and a hot walk home, he and his father would return to the cluster of white houses in the coolness of approaching evening to rejoin the busy little world within the courtyard.

Things always seemed to come to life again once the midday heat was past. Pigeons would flutter and coo in the dovecote. Welcome breezes would stir the striped awnings that hung over the doorways of the houses. Children would run this way and that, laughing, playing, chasing the goats and chickens, kicking up the dust. It was like that now, and it made him miss his father even more.

"Hi, Andrew!" bubbled Lyra as she burst from the door of their house. She darted past him and ran straight to the old gray goat, whose neck she patted and hugged with obvious affection. "I'm going to teach old Baal to pull a cart. What do you think?"

"Whatever," said Andrew, stuffing his cap into his belt.

It was nearly a month now since his father had gone away. No one in the village had seen him during that time, though everyone pretended to have the latest information on his whereabouts. Once two travelers, beaten and bloody, had passed through on their way to Gadara. They claimed that a wild man, naked, savage, and incredibly strong, had attacked them on the steep path at south end of the lake. Some of the villagers had laughed at them. A few had warned them severely never to go near the Haunts of the Dead again. But most had simply nodded and exchanged knowing glances. "Crazy Jacob," they said.

There were all kinds of rumors, of course. Some said Jacob had lost his mind because he was a Jew who denied the power of the *real* gods. Others were certain that he had sold his soul to Chemosh and Temaz or that the spirits of the dead had taken possession of his body. Still others claimed that he was a conjurer whose spells had backfired. Whatever the reason, Jacob bar Hosep, master boatwright, originally of Magdala across Kinneret, had lost his mind and was living like a beast among the cave tombs on the side of the cliff. And everyone knew it.

Andrew was sitting there on the crate wondering what it all meant when his mother, laying aside her shuttle, came over and touched his hand. "Did you stop on the way home?"

"Yes," he answered. "I took the basket of bread and fish, too. Left it in the cave—the same one we sat in together during that storm."

"Did you see him?"

"No. But I . . . heard things."

Helena sighed. Then, removing her head covering and pushing a few curls of dark hair away from her face, she untied a soft leather purse that hung from her girdle and handed it to Andrew.

"This is all we have left," she said. "I'll have more cloth to sell in Gadara by the end of the week. But we're out of grain and oil and I need them to bake our bread. There are still a few hours of daylight left. Can you go into the town and buy some for me?"

"Won't the merchants be closed?"

"Not until sunset. You'll have time if you go quickly."

"I'll run!" said Andrew, getting to his feet and taking the purse from her hand. He was pleased to have some way of helping her.

"Can I go too?" begged Lyra. "Me and old Baal?"

"Not this time, Lyra," said Helena. "Andrew is in a hurry."

She bent to kiss his cheek. "Be swift, my son." After a pause, she quickly added, "And may the gods go with you."

Andrew stopped halfway to the gate. "Mother," he said, "is it the gods and spirits who have made Father this way?"

She shook her head. "I don't know, Andrew."

"Well, if it is, do you think there might be a way to get them to make him better again?"

"I know very little about the gods and spirits," she answered. "To tell you the truth, I'm sick of the whole subject. As far as I can see, no good has ever come of it. I don't know what it would take to make him well," she added wearily. "Some kind of a miracle, I suppose."

A miracle, he thought. *I wonder if Stephen would know . . .*

"Goodbye, Mother!" he called, replacing his cap on the top of his head. "I'll be back as soon as I can!"

Then he ran out at the gate, leaving a flurry of squawking chickens and flying feathers behind him.

Gadara. Its roofs and columns glowed pink in the light of the setting sun as Andrew trotted down the dusty road toward the city's northwest gate. The sun had not yet dipped below the silhouetted summit of Mount Moreh in the west. He should be able to make it in plenty of time. *And when I'm done*, he thought, *I'll find Stephen. Stephen seems to know something about the power of the gods and spirits.*

There was nothing else in Andrew's experience that could even compare with Gadara. The *agora,* or market-place; the temples; the gymnasium; the stadium; the wide paved streets crowded with people and horses and carts and chariots; the scholars and statesmen and dignitaries in their flowing white togas—he loved it all. The trip to Gadara, which he had made many times with his father, never failed to stir his imagination.

It was about three miles from Andrew's village to the city—a distance he could cover in a surprisingly short time by walking and running in turns. He was used to it. Like most people of the trades and laboring classes, Andrew went everywhere on foot.

Heavy traffic caused him to slacken his pace as he approached the gate. The people on the road slowed to a stop as from somewhere behind them there came a trumpet blast. The crowd divided. A red-bearded seller of purple fabric pulled Andrew out of the road. "Legionaries coming through!" he said.

Andrew stood gaping as a troop of 100 Roman soldiers—members, he knew, of the Fourteenth Legion—marched into the town. It was an awe-inspiring sight. Everything about the Romans was terrible and impressive: their brassy armor, their bright-red tunics, their flashing spear points, their square jaws set tightly within the leather cheek guards of their helmets. *What must it be like to see an entire Legion marching together? Six thousand men and their weapons!* It was no wonder, Andrew reflected, that Rome had mastered the world.

When the soldiers had passed and the people were moving again, Andrew stepped within the shadow of the gate. Once under the archway, he paused to glance up at the familiar images carved there: the golden eagle, symbol of imperial Rome, flashing red in the dying light; below that, Olympian Zeus (or Baal, as some of the local people said), riding on a rain cloud and gripping thunderbolts in his fist; last of all, a nameless, grinning daemon his father had always called lucky Meonen. *Maybe not so lucky after all*, Andrew thought.

Skillfully picking his way through the jostling donkeys, carts, merchants, and farmers, Andrew emerged inside the city walls. Ahead of him stretched a canyonlike street of close-clustered two-story buildings. At its end he glimpsed the bright awnings of the booths in the *agora*. Avoiding the muddy gutter that trickled down the middle of the pavement, he took off at a run in the direction of the marketplace.

He was only two houses away when a bulky figure emerged from a narrow side lane and stopped him cold.

"Well, now! If it isn't the Jew boy!" jeered a painfully familiar voice. A chorus of laughter followed.

Demas.

Behind the apprentice lurked seven or eight other boys. Andrew recognized a couple of them from his days at the academy. He guessed the others were swineherds from the pasturelands that lay between Gadara and Lake Kinneret—all of them dirty, scruffy, and mean-looking.

"*Bar Meshugga!*" taunted a tall, hollow-cheeked boy dressed only in a soiled linen tunic.

"That's Jew talk, in case you didn't know," teased a stocky little fellow with thick black hair. "It means 'son of a lunatic.' "

More laughs.

"What are you doing here, Demas?" said Andrew.

"Me? Just working out the details with Uncle Artemas," the big boy replied. "About my new job."

"New job?"

"You heard me. Herding pigs on the plateau above the cliff."

"But you can't do that! Stephen needs your help!"

"Can," smirked Demas. "And *will*. Uncle Artemas says your old boat business is finished anyhow. And good riddance!"

"Oh, yeah?"

"Yeah!" laughed one of the pig boys. "Crazy Jacob's Boat Brigade."

"Shut up!" said Andrew, making a fist with his right hand.

"Crazy Jacob! Crazy Jacob!" a few of the boys began to chant.

"Stop it!"

"He *is* crazy!" said the black-haired boy. "I know, 'cause I seen him with *no clothes on!*"

Everyone laughed again. Then they all took up the refrain:

> Crazy Jacob! Crazy man!
> Lost his robe and away he ran!
> Danced in the sun till he got a tan!
> Dance, crazy Jacob!

Before he knew what he was doing, Andrew was on top of Demas. His fist was in the air, poised to slam itself into the quivering pink flesh of the round, pudgy face. But before he could strike, two or three of the other boys pulled him off and threw him to the ground. There they pinned him while Demas lumbered to his feet.

"Well, now. *That* was a mistake," said Demas, feigning coolness but trembling violently. "When I get through with you, you're gonna—"

He stopped, catching sight of Andrew's purse. "Oho! What's *this?*"

"Leave it alone!" yelled Andrew, struggling to free himself. Demas bent down and yanked the purse from its cord.

"Jingle, jingle, jingle!" sang Demas, shaking the little bag of silver coins. "Looks like lucky Meonen's on *my* side now!"

Andrew twisted and turned. "You give that back!"

"*Demas!*" came a man's voice from the other side of the street. "Drop that and let him go! *Now!*"

The purse fell. The boys all jumped up and ran. Andrew sat up and looked.

It was Stephen.

CHAPTER 6

Stephen!" At that moment Andrew felt as if he'd never been so glad to see anybody in his whole life.

"Demas trouble?" asked Stephen, helping the boy to his feet and brushing the dust from his cloak and tunic.

" 'Crazy Jacob' trouble," Andrew responded, fumbling to reattach the leather purse to his belt.

"I see. And what brings you to town so late in the day?"

"Mother needs grain and oil tonight or we won't have any bread tomorrow. This is the last of our money," he added, patting the leather purse.

"The last!" said Stephen, raising his bushy eyebrows. "That won't do! Here, I have a few coins of my own left—enough to buy her an extra measure of barley, I think. But we'd better do it quickly. The shopmen are packing up to go home."

The grain merchant grumbled about having to reopen a sack of wheat that he had already loaded on his donkey for the trip home. Yet he showed no lack of eagerness when it came to taking Andrew's money.

The shadows were lengthening over the *agora* and a dry wind was sporting in the shop awnings when they set out for home. It would be dark by the time they reached the village. But then a walk under the stars on a summer evening would be pleasant, especially with the black-eyed Greek as a traveling companion. *This will be my chance to ask him*, Andrew thought.

"Thanks, Stephen," he said as they came out of the gate and set foot upon the road. "Again."

"Well," laughed his friend, "it's just lucky I happened to be there!"

"Lucky," mused Andrew, glancing up at the leering gargoyle above the gate. "Like old Meonen. Maybe he *was* watching out for me, after all."

"You mean you'd begun to doubt it?" asked Stephen.

"Haven't *you?*" returned Andrew, staring back at him. "I mean, Meonen was always sort of a favorite of my father's."

"Ah, yes. I see."

Far to the west, out where Andrew knew the Great Sea stretched away to the end of the earth, the sky was aflame with orange, copper, and violet. Above the craggy ridges to the east the horned moon sailed like a *dancing ship*. Andrew and Stephen quickened their pace as they felt the darkness gathering.

"Stephen," said Andrew in a little while, "you believe

in the gods and spirits, don't you? As my father does . . .
I mean, *did?*"

"Perhaps. Perhaps not quite in the same way."

"In what way, then?"

"That's difficult to say," Stephen replied after a
thoughtful pause. "I suppose I'm a little bit like Plato."

"Plato?"

"One of our greatest thinkers—the Greeks', I mean.
You would have heard about him if you'd stayed on at
the academy."

"Really? Could you introduce me to him?"

"No, no, no!" laughed Stephen. "He died about 400
years ago! But he wrote things about our Greek gods that
would make you think he both *believed* and *didn't* believe in them."

"How could he do that?"

"I'm not sure. I think he believed in them as pictures
or shadows of . . . well, I don't know—some greater
God, maybe. The one true God. Sort of like the God of
your father's people."

Something inside Andrew perked up at this. "Do you
believe in Yahweh, then? The God of the Jews?"

"I've often wondered," Stephen replied.

They walked on into the hazy distance as Ishtar and
K'siyl—Venus and Orion to the Greeks and Romans—
began to twinkle in the blue dome above their heads.
After a while, Andrew said, "What about miracles?"

"Hmmm?"

"Miracles. Do you think that the gods—or the one true God, whoever He is—cause things to happen? Like making sick people get well?"

Stephen stroked his smooth chin and was silent a moment. Then he answered, "A few weeks ago I think I'd have said no. And yet . . ."—here he paused, putting his face very close to Andrew's and lowering his voice—"I've been hearing stories about happenings of that very sort. On the other side of the lake."

Andrew's mouth dropped open. "Who told you?" he said, surprised at the eagerness in his own voice.

"Fishermen. From Capernaum. One of them said that his wife's mother had been cured of a fever—just like that!—by a man named Jesus."

They walked on in silence while Andrew's imagination burned with the things Stephen had told him. When at last the lights of the village appeared at the end of their road—flickering strangely, it seemed—Andrew said, "Stephen, do you think there might be anyone like this Jesus on *our* side of the lake?"

"I couldn't say for certain. I'm not sure what kind of a man he is. There are the conjurers, of course—"

"Conjurers?"

"Magicians. Wizards. All the old women swear by them."

"Do you know where I can find any of them?"

Stephen eyed him oddly in the light of the moon and stars. "At the Place of the Stone," he said. "Near Philoteria, where the Jordan leaves Kinneret—the place the ancients called Beth Yerah, the House of the Moon." He paused. "Are you going to tell your mother?"

"Tell my mother—?" Andrew began. But then he stopped in midsentence and pointed. "Stephen, look!"

They were now close enough to see the cause of the odd flickering of the light from the village. Fire!

They ran the rest of the way to the cluster of houses, dashing into the courtyard just in time to see several men beating out the last of the flames with leather tarps. It was a scene of complete confusion. Men coughed and hacked and waved their arms and cloaks at the thick smoke. Children, goats, and chickens ran this way and that, crying, bleating, and clucking. Women came and went between the ring of houses and the well, pouring water on the smoldering heap, then hurrying away to refill their jars. The donkey stamped and brayed.

It seemed the fire had begun in the straw around the donkey's manger and spread along the wall of one of the houses. That wall was badly blackened but still standing. The awning seemed to have had the worst of it. It was now nothing more than a flutter of smoking black ribbons. Andrew breathed a sigh of relief. It could have been so much worse.

Through the smoke he caught sight of his mother

standing by the door of their house with Lyra in her arms. He ran to her at once.

"Your father," said Helena, looking not at Andrew but at the blackened wall. "He was here."

"Father did this?" exclaimed Andrew.

"What happened?" asked Stephen, stepping up and laying a hand on Helena's arm.

"Something I would not have believed unless I had seen it with my own eyes," she answered. "I was working at the loom when I saw him run into the courtyard. Naked, filthy—like a . . . a *beast!* I picked up Lyra and ran with her into the house—I didn't want him to frighten her again. When I returned, he was standing at the open door of the big brick oven. I saw him reach in-side. He took out a coal—a coal as hot and glowing as the fire in his eyes—and just stood there with it, holding it in the palm of his hand! He didn't even seem to feel it. I screamed. He looked up at me—I think I startled him—and dropped the coal. It rolled into a pile of straw. Then he ran away. That's all." She bent her head and laid her cheek against the hair of the little girl who lay sobbing on her shoulder.

"I'm afraid that *isn't* all," said a high-pitched, nasal voice. Andrew turned to see the short, round shape of Artemas. The wispy black whiskers around his thick lips waved in the air as he nodded in greeting.

"As a matter of fact," Artemas went on, "this is

probably just the beginning. There is sure to be more of the same . . . unless measures are taken." He smiled unpleasantly.

Andrew felt the muscles of his jaw tensing.

"What kind of measures?" asked Stephen.

"I wouldn't like to guess," the herdsman responded. "*Extreme* measures, no doubt. I mean to speak with the authorities in the morning. The man is out of his mind. Dangerous. A menace to the community. Something *has* to be done."

"But he's my father!" said Andrew.

"Unfortunately, yes," agreed Artemas, pulling his tasseled cloak over his head. "A good evening to you all." He smiled, nodded, and walked out of the courtyard.

Helena sat down on a stone with Lyra on her lap. "What do you think he means, Stephen?"

Stephen brooded silently, staring at the remains of the fire.

"He's right about one thing, the old pork-face!" said Andrew. "Something *has* to be done! And it *will* be done—*tonight!*" Catching up a walking staff that was leaning against the doorpost, he wrapped his own cloak around himself and turned to follow Artemas out the gate.

"Andrew!" his mother called after him. "There's nothing you can do, especially not tonight! Where do you think you're you going?"

"The House of the Moon" was his only answer.

CHAPTER 7

Beth Yerah, or House of the Moon, lay at the extreme southwest tip of the lake, near a marshy place where the waters of Galilee flowed into the River Jordan. Andrew had heard his father speak of it more than once. In those early days, Jacob had said, long before Joshua and Israel had entered the land, Beth Yerah had been a shrine dedicated to the worship of the moon god, Sin. Andrew couldn't help wondering what kind of god Sin might be as he trekked over the dark, rocky landscape, staff in hand, with the light of the thumbnail moon glinting on the darkened face of the lake. *Maybe Sin can help my father*, Andrew thought.

The night was deep and far spent by the time he reached a ridge from which he could see the town of Philoteria lying in the distance across the river. Much closer, down in a reedy hollow at his feet, stood the black shape of a huge boulder. Andrew stopped and leaned on his walking staff, staring down at the dark mass, wondering what he should do next. Suddenly, a hand touched his shoulder. He jumped.

"You found it!" whispered a voice at his ear.

"Stephen!" gasped Andrew, falling against his friend and grabbing his arm. "You nearly scared me to death!"

Stephen laughed. "Sorry. I followed you. Couldn't let you come alone." He shrugged. "Not while your mother was watching, anyhow. I promised her that if I couldn't stop you, I'd at least keep an eye on you." He grinned in the moony darkness.

Andrew pointed to the dark shape in the hollow. "The Place of the Stone?"

Stephen nodded. "The one and only. They *live* there, from what I'm told. Around on the other side of the rock."

"*Live* there?"

"Yes." With a sweep of his arm, Stephen indicated the downward path. "Shall we?"

"Why not?" gulped Andrew. He shook himself, gripped his staff tightly, and stepped down the slope, determined to do whatever was needed to find help for his father.

It was slow going. Together they slogged and squelched their way through the muck, pushing tall reeds aside and slipping on slimy stones. Once Andrew had to stop to retrieve a sandal that got stuck in the mud. But before long they had rounded the shoulder of the huge rock and stood facing a large hole that gaped like an open mouth in its western face. *Great*, thought Andrew. *Just what I need. Another cave.*

He stood hesitating in the wet gravel outside the cave's entrance. He could feel his heart pounding in his chest as he looked down into the hole. Everything about it was black. The smoke stains around its edges, the empty spaces inside, even the feelings it stirred inside him as he stood in front of it were black. *What now?* Andrew didn't know how to speak to a conjurer, whether to cry out or strike the rocky doorway with his walking stick or repeat some kind of spell . . . or turn and flee.

Then he heard voices. "Somebody's in there!" he whispered.

"Of course somebody's in there!" said Stephen. "Isn't that why we came?" Raising his voice, the Greek called out, "Hello? Anybody home?"

Andrew gaped at his greeting. Stephen shrugged.

More sounds. Someone was coming. A dark shape appeared in the doorway.

"Who is it? Who, who indeed?" croaked a thin, dry voice—a voice as dry and crackling as the dead reeds surrounding the entrance to the cave.

Stephen gave Andrew a nudge. "Speak up!" he said.

Andrew cleared his throat and stepped forward. "I've, uh, come to see the conjurers. Are you one of them?"

"One of two! One of three! One of four! One of many!" crackled the dry voice. "Who wants to know? Who wants to know?"

"Andrew. Son of Jacob the boatwright."

A light flickered and flared. In the glow of a hand-held clay lamp a face appeared—an old woman's face, yellow, long, furrowed, and skull-like, with a narrow, pointed chin and barely any nose at all. It was surrounded by stray tufts of gray hair and set deep within the shadowy folds of a woolen cloak.

"Step in," said the woman, ushering them into a dank chamber that looked as if it had been hewn out of the rock. *Like the Haunts of the Dead*, thought Andrew, shivering. The place was strewn with bleached bones, broken pottery, cold ashes, and row upon row of sealed stone jars. Andrew wondered how the bones had got there. Were they animal bones? Human? A chill crawled up his back and he quickly looked away.

"Who is it, Anath?" said another voice—this one sleepy and deep-toned—from the inner recesses of the cave.

"A boy. A man. A man and a boy," answered Anath, squinting at Andrew and Stephen through the smoke. She set her lamp on a ledge of rock and unceremoniously seated herself on the floor. "Company! Customers! Come out, Enkidu! Come out!"

A man, elderly but straight and tall, stepped into the

light. He, too, was cloaked in gray. His hair was thick and white. Around his neck hung a long gold chain from which dangled countless silver pendants and amulets— star shapes, crescent moons, spearlike sunbeams, serpents, grinning demons. Unlike the old crone, the man had a full, round face. He almost looked kindly. He yawned, glanced absently from Andrew to Stephen, then from Stephen to Anath.

"What is it?" he said. "A man needs his sleep."

"No time for sleep!" scoffed the old woman, picking up a small bone and twirling it between her fingers. "They are wanting something from old Anath and Enkidu, I think. Yes?"

Andrew gulped and nodded. He tried to speak, but his tongue felt like a wad of wool. His knees began to buckle. Supporting himself on his staff, he leaned forward and opened his mouth. "My father," he heard himself say in a voice nearly as thin and dry as Anath's own, "—he's gone crazy! Because of the spirits or the gods or something. He's living in the tombs, the Haunts of the Dead."

"The Haunts of the Dead!" whispered Enkidu. His forehead lifted into a series of wrinkles. He stuck out his lips and whistled. Anath grinned and nodded.

"Yes," said Andrew, taking courage. "The Haunts of the Dead. He runs around naked and beats people up.

He started a fire in our village. He held a hot coal in his bare hand!"

The two conjurers turned and stared at one another. Then in unison they pronounced a single name: *"Chashmagoz!"*

"Can you help him?" pleaded Andrew. "Can you make him better? Can Sin, the god of the moon, do anything for him?"

Anath and Enkidu smiled. "It all depends," said the hag. "Have you brought *keseph?"*

"Keseph?" Andrew darted a confused glance at Stephen. "Money? But I don't have—"

By way of response, Stephen reached inside his cloak, pulled a small bag of coins from his belt, and tossed it to the floor. It landed with a chink in front of the two magicians. "I had a feeling we'd need it," he said.

Old Enkidu beamed. His baubles jangled and his rich white hair gleamed in the lamplight as he leaned forward, picked up the purse, and tucked it safely inside his own robe. Then, with a sudden change of expression, he folded his hands, closed his heavy-lidded eyes, and frowned gravely. "Plainly a case of fire demons," he said.

"Fire demons?" echoed Andrew.

"Plainly?" said Stephen dryly.

"Most certainly," said Anath, bobbing her head up and down so vigorously that the whole of her bony frame shook with it.

"Chashmagoz, chief of the demons, demands appeasement," continued the old man.

"Yes, indeed," agreed the hag. "Sacrifice."

Sacrifice? Andrew squirmed uneasily.

"But we will subdue him by the power of Sin, god of the moon."

"Subdue him, yes! But only at great cost!"

"*That* part I can believe," muttered Stephen.

"Then you can help us?" Andrew asked hopefully.

"Can—and will—yes, indeed," croaked Anath.

"Tomorrow," affirmed Enkidu, opening his eyes. "We will meet you tomorrow at the Haunts of the Dead. At moonrise."

"Moonrise," repeated the old crone. She smacked her lips and wagged her narrow chin from side to side within the folds of her robe. Then her toothless grin faded and she scowled. "Now go!" she said, pointing a bony finger at the door.

With that, Stephen grabbed Andrew by the arm and almost dragged him from the cave. In a moment the two of them were standing once again on the mushy gravel outside the entrance. The sliver of moon had passed the zenith and was bending its course toward the west. The darkness of the marsh and the heights above lay before them. Andrew leaned on Stephen and breathed a sigh of relief.

"My feelings exactly," said the Greek.

"Tomorrow night, then?" said Andrew, giving his friend a tentative look.

"Yes," said Stephen. "Tomorrow at moonrise we shall see just how much power Sin really has."

CHAPTER 8

The following day was one long agony of waiting. From sunup till sundown, Andrew and Stephen labored beside Lake Kinneret's sparkling waters, just as they did every day.

Without Demas's help, it had been necessary to put in long hours and exert extra effort just to complete the boats Jacob had promised to his customers. It was no longer a question of finishing on time but of finishing at all. But even with so many other tasks to be done, Andrew still somehow found time to continue working on his own boat. That, he felt, was something he simply couldn't give up.

And he had made good progress, too. By this time, the hull was finished. Edge to edge, Andrew had joined the cedar planks, fitting every tenon snugly into its mortise, just as his father had taught him. Every seam was as smooth and as tight as he could possibly make it. Now it was simply a matter of inserting the oak frame, securing it to the sides with more wooden pegs and brass nails, installing a bench or two, and brushing on a couple of stiff, heavy coats of pitch.

Andrew took great pleasure in the work. He saw it as his last link with the man who now wandered wild and naked somewhere among the tombs on the side of the cliff.

When it was dark enough for the first stars to appear, Andrew turned toward the rugged eastern horizon and saw the sickle moon poke the tip of one bright point up into the darkness. From the surface of the lake an evening mist arose. He and Stephen exchanged looks. It was time.

They took the narrow trail up the side of the cliff. As they wound their way higher and higher, Andrew had a curious feeling that the darkness and dampness were following close behind, clinging to the hem of his cloak and tickling his heels. Looking over his shoulder, he saw that the fog was indeed making its way up the cliff, quickly covering that part of the path they had already traveled. He felt his chest tighten as they approached the curve in the trail where the first of the cave tombs gaped among the rocks. He tried to put out of his mind the deep, black holes that contained the rotting bones. He tried to ignore his certainty that they were full of watching eyes. But he couldn't fool his stomach, which churned within him.

"Stay close, now," Stephen called back to him. "I don't want to lose you in the fog."

"I wish we knew exactly where they were planning to meet us," said Andrew, shivering involuntarily. "They never even—"

He was cut off by a shriek like the cry of a frightened or wounded beast. He and Stephen covered their heads as a small shower of rocks and gravel poured down over them from above.

"What was that?" whispered Andrew after a tense pause.

"*Ssshh!*" warned Stephen. "Keep still! Might be a jackal or—"

Suddenly a bony hand touched Andrew's shoulder. He gasped and whirled around.

"Moonrise—yes, indeed," croaked a thin, dry voice at his ear.

"And the patient is nearby, I assume?" added a second voice, calm, complacent, and vaguely sleepy.

"He *must* be close!" breathed Andrew to Anath and Enkidu once he had regained control of his voice. His heart pounded as if it would burst. "We know he's living here among the tombs. Do you think you can find him?"

"He won't be easy to catch," offered Stephen, peering at the two conjurers through the thickening mist and darkness.

"Catch? Don't have to catch—no, indeed," cackled the old woman, bouncing up and down on her toes.

"Certainly not," agreed Enkidu with a warm,

assuring chuckle. "No need to get any closer than this. Why take unnecessary risks?" A pleasant smile spread over his broad, kindly face.

"Seriously?" asked Stephen. "You mean you don't need to see him or touch him or—?"

"No! No touching! Too dangerous!" said Anath, squinting and shaking her head. "Just *spells*. Watch."

From under the folds of her cloak, she drew a piece of flint and a long, knobby stick of wood covered with thick, black tar at one end. Striking the flint against the rocky face of the cliff, she lit the torch. In a few moments it was flaring out brazenly against the surrounding darkness. Immediately there came another animal-like cry from above.

"Hmm," said Enkidu, raising his sparse eyebrows. "Perhaps we had better proceed quickly."

"Indeed!" agreed his partner, cocking an ear toward the cliff.

With his right hand, the old man fumbled in the folds of his own gown and produced an amber-colored glass vial. From this he poured a small amount of white powder.

"What's that?" asked Andrew.

In answer, Enkidu tossed the powder into the flame of Anath's torch. Andrew flinched as the fire flashed bright red, then green, then blue. Through the thick white smoke that followed, he gazed upward, searching for any sign of movement among the rocks.

"Incense! Good, good, good!" cackled the hag. "And now the *sacrifice!*" From a sack that hung within her outer garment, she pulled out something stiff and fuzzy and strangely odorous.

"A dead cat!" gasped Andrew.

"That's a sacrifice?" mumbled Stephen.

"In the name of Sin!" shrieked the crone, hurling the carcass up the side of the cliff.

Enkidu smiled and patted Andrew's shoulder.

Then, as Andrew watched, the old woman started bobbing from side to side. She lifted her hands above her head, splayed her fingers wide, and padded her feet upon the pathway in an odd, rhythmic dance. Enkidu joined in, shaking his pendants and amulets and humming a single low note. Then he produced a small tambourine and began beating on it slowly. Together, the two conjurers chanted:

> *Agrath, Azelath, Asiya,*
> *Amarlai, Sharlai, Belusiya!*
> *Burst and curse! Dash and ban*
> *Chashmagoz, Merigoz from this man!*

Andrew stood entranced. Never in his life had he seen such a display. The fire, the smoke, the mysterious words—all of it made a deep impression upon him. *This will do the trick!* he thought, a surge of hope rising within him. *This will save Father! If this won't do it, then nothing—"*

Crash!

A small avalanche of dirt and rock rained down on the little group. A horrendous howl pierced the night. Something as fierce and powerful as a lion from the Jordan thickets exploded off the ledge above them and threw itself on top of old Enkidu.

"*Aagghhh!* Off! Off!" the old man cried as he fell. The tambourine bounced on the path and jangled away into the mist.

"Not *me!*" shrieked Anath, flinging her arms skyward and casting the torch aside. It plummeted down the cliff, briefly illuminating the bleak rocks below before snuffing itself in the swirling fog. "Help, O Sin!" she screamed, frantically wedging her skinny body into a narrow space between two large stones. "Murder! Death! Betrayal!"

Trembling, Andrew edged his way along the path away from all the confusion, darkness, cries, and thrashing of arms and legs. The mist around his head filled with screams and snarls and dull, thudding sounds. Where was Stephen? Had he been able to escape? Andrew couldn't wait around to find out. He crept along until he felt an empty space open up in the side of the cliff. One of the caves. Gasping for breath, he backed into the hole and fell to his hands and knees just inside the entrance. Then he waited to see what would happen next.

As he listened, the scuffle reached a climax, then suddenly ended with a chilling screech. This was followed by the sounds of feet scrabbling hurriedly down the gravel path, and the howls of the two conjurers fading into the murky distance below.

When everything was still, Andrew called, "Stephen!" Cautiously, he stuck his head out of the cavern to listen. *"Stephen!* Are you there?" A moment later, he heard footsteps, followed by a cough and a groan.

"Andrew?" Stephen replied in a weak voice.

"Here! I'm here!"

Stephen approached slowly and painfully. His cloak was gone. His tunic was half torn from his upper body. The right side of his face was covered with blood that streamed from a gash above his eyebrow. He stumbled to the opening of the cavern and leaned against it.

"Was it a lion?" Andrew asked, afraid of the truth.

"It was your father," Stephen said.

CHAPTER 9

Jesus.

He could not get that name out of his mind. Over and over, it pushed its way to the top of his brain as he prepared to launch his newly finished boat on the waters of Kinneret. Again and again, Stephen's words replayed themselves in his memory: "stories about happenings of that very sort" . . . "on the other side of the lake" . . . "cured of a fever" . . . "a man named Jesus". . . .

Nearby stood little Lyra with old Baal and his cart. She had two fingers in her mouth and a strand of brown hair across her nose. Her brown eyes were wide with wonder at the spectacle unfolding on the shore.

"They're just pigs," Andrew said with disgust, grunting as he untied the ropes and prepared to push the boat into the water.

Over the lake, small birds wheeled and chirped, their peaceful existence shattered for the moment by the squeals of the animals on the beach. Dogs barked. Boys shouted and waved sticks in an attempt to herd the pigs through the shallow water, up a plank, and onto a large boat anchored just off shore.

"Swine for Susita and Gergesa," Andrew heard a high-pitched, nasal voice say. Glancing up, he saw Artemas standing a few feet away, broad and impressive in a black robe and white turban. He handed a papyrus scroll to the boat's grizzled captain.

"*Mmmph.*" The captain unrolled the scroll and studied it. "Lucky for you, that's where I'm goin'."

"I expect they'll fetch a handsome price," the pig farmer went on smilingly. "You'll have your share, of course, when we settle accounts."

"Nobody gets nothin' unless those pigs get on the boat," said the captain, spitting in the sand and eyeing the boys at their work.

"We *will* be needing a reliable agent on the northeast shore," Artemas added with a wink. "There are lots more where these came from—all growing fat up on the plateau." He jerked a thumb at the cliffs.

"Fat," said the captain. "I can believe that."

Suddenly Andrew felt himself being shoved from behind. He pitched forward and fell into the boat. Lyra squealed. The herding boys laughed.

"Nice boat, *Bar Meshugga.* Is it for your little sister?"

Andrew scrambled to his feet. "Shut up, Demas!" he said.

"Too bad it's not big enough to carry any of Uncle

Artemas's pigs up to the northeast shore. That's where the *real* money is. But you poor people wouldn't know anything about that, would you?"

Andrew climbed out of the boat and turned away.

"How's your old man these days?" Demas persisted with mock concern. "Finding his chains comfortable? *Hmmm?*"

"Demas!" shouted Artemas. "Get back to work!"

"Yes, Uncle! See you later, *Bar Meshugga*—in a cave somewhere, probably, with crazy Jacob!" Demas and his companions moved off.

"Come on, Lyra," said Andrew. "Let's go help Mother."

He took her by the hand and trudged up the beach to meet Helena and Stephen, who were headed down to the boat with armloads of yarn and cloth to sell on the other side of the lake. Andrew's jaw tensed at the thought of Demas's taunts. It was too much! His father—with iron shackles on his wrists, fetters on his ankles, chained to the bare rock. *And all because of Artemas*, he thought bitterly.

It was true. After Enkidu and Anath had run screaming into the village, babbling about the "madman on the cliff," Artemas had lost no time in bringing in the city authorities. Soldiers from Gadara had hunted Jacob down, bound him hand and foot, chained him to the cliffside, and left him to die.

"What was that all about?" asked Helena as she approached.

"Oh, just Demas," said Andrew. "He thinks he's so tough and smart! What he doesn't know is that father *broke* those stupid chains last night. And I sure won't tell him."

Stephen whistled. "Broke them *again?*"

Helena shook her head. Then she turned to Lyra. "Now you mind Stephen while Andrew and I are gone," she said, laying her fabrics inside the boat and stooping to kiss the little girl's head. "We'll be spending the night with Aunt Hadassah and Uncle Yohanan in Capernaum."

"Yes, Mother," said Lyra. "I'll make sure old Baal minds too."

Stephen laughed. "You two had better be on your way," he said.

Together they pushed the little boat into the shallows. Andrew watched as Stephen took his mother by the arm and helped her in. Then he, too, jumped aboard, grabbed the oars, and took his place on the rowing bench.

"I hope you sell every last bit of it," said Stephen, touching Helena's hand. Andrew didn't like that. "May the gods—" the Greek hesitated, then winced and gingerly put a finger to the scar above his eye. "May *good luck* go with you."

"We could use it," said Helena with a sigh. "There's

not much hope of selling anything on *this* side of the lake anymore."

Stephen shoved them out into the deeper water. "Good-bye," he called. "And Helena, think about what I've said."

"I will," answered Andrew's mother.

Andrew stared back at Stephen, puzzling over the meaning of his words. Then he bent to the oars as Lyra waved from the beach.

The little craft bounced over the waves like a cork. Suddenly, in spite of everything—his father's madness, his mother's fears, the family's growing burden of poverty—it was a glorious day. The sun shone like gold. The blue water sparkled. It was his boat's maiden voyage! *A dancing ship*, he thought excitedly. *She really does dance! And I built her myself!* Jacob would be proud—but as he remembered the night in the cave, Andrew wasn't sure what his father would have said about this trip. *I'm not exactly alone*, he thought. *Mother is with me.*

"Mother," he wondered aloud as his oars beat the water and the waves slapped the sides of the boat, "why didn't Father want me to go out alone in my boat?"

She regarded him gravely. "Did he tell you that?"

A dark cloud crossed his face. "Yes. I never told you, but the first time I mentioned it . . . well, *that* was when he started to go crazy. So I've always kind of felt like this whole thing was *my* fault."

Helena frowned. Her dark eyes grew a shade darker. She reached over and put a hand on his shoulder. "It's not your fault," she said.

"Your father," she continued in a moment, "when he was a boy in Magdala, had a younger brother. Benjamin. They learned the craft of boat-building from *their* father. They were always together, working in the shop, fishing, sailing on the water. Jacob loved his brother. One day there came a storm. Benjamin was out on the lake alone in a small boat, like this one. He never came back."

Andrew stared. Not once had he heard a word about this part of his father's history.

"Your father cried out to his people's God, to Yahweh. He prayed that *his* life might be taken in exchange for Benjamin's. But his brother did not return. So Jacob grew angry. And afraid. In time, his fear and anger grew into bitterness. When he was old enough, he left his people and came to live on our side of the lake. When I met him, I grew to love him. He was quiet, gentle but strong, and he seemed to feel things very deeply. In time, we were married. But I never understood why he felt so strongly about the gods and spirits, why he feared them so much and tried so hard to avoid angering them, until he told me about Benjamin."

Jesus. The name whispered itself to him once again. Was the God of Jesus the same as the God of the Jews? Stephen had heard such marvelous things about this man

Jesus. And yet the God of the Jews had failed to answer his father's prayers.

"Mother," Andrew said again after he had been rowing in silence for what seemed a very long time, "what did Stephen say?"

"Stephen?" she said, looking up abruptly. Andrew thought he saw a hint of color in her cheeks.

"He asked you to think about something."

She cast her eyes down again. She seemed embarrassed to tell him. "Andrew," she said, "Stephen is concerned about us. A woman alone with two children. He sees how we are struggling."

"So?"

"He has offered to marry me."

"Marry you!"

"Yes."

"But he *can't* marry you!"

"Why not? You like Stephen, don't you?"

"Of course I like Stephen! But he's not my father! He *can't* be!"

"Andrew—" she faltered. "It is hard to live with so much shame. And what about the money? What about the bread? What about Lyra?"

Andrew scowled at her. "If you marry Stephen, what happens when Father gets well?"

She tried to smile but couldn't. Tears welled up in her

eyes. "Your father—" she began, then broke off. "I just don't think—"

"But he *will!*" Andrew shouted. "He will get well!" It was the last word either of them spoke until they reached the other side of the lake.

Aunt Hadassah and Uncle Yohanan were waiting for them when they came to shore in Capernaum. Uncle Yohanan helped them unload the bolts of fabric and hanks of yarn and bring them to the marketplace. Aunt Hadassah arranged for Helena to spend the day selling her wares at the cloth merchants' booth. For an hour or two, Andrew worked with them, carrying the fabrics to the stand and spreading them out on the display racks. Then, when it seemed that his help was no longer needed, he quietly slipped away.

Stephen marry Mother? he thought as he ran through the marketplace. He couldn't imagine such a thing. Andrew might as well let Lyra sail his boat!

He knew now what had to be done. He dashed past the covered merchants' booths, dodging carts and donkeys, hopping over baskets of fruit and vegetables, avoiding collisions with buyers and sellers. He searched the face of every man, woman, and child he passed, looking for someone who might be able to answer the question that was burning in his heart and mind. At last he saw a group of fishermen coming up from the beach. *Fishermen. From Capernaum.* With a sudden burst of determination, he ran straight up to them.

"Please," he said, grasping the sleeve of the first one, "do you know where I can find the man called Jesus?"

The big fisherman turned and looked down at him. "Follow me," he said and strode off.

CHAPTER 10

Andrew's heart sank. "In *there?*" he said. "How am I ever going to get in *there?*"

The little white house was bursting with people—people standing, people sitting, people jammed into the doorway, people clinging to the latticework shutters of the two small windows. Never had Andrew seen such a big crowd in such a small place.

"Who said anything about getting in?" said the big fisherman at his elbow. "I only promised to take you where you could find Him."

"His own mother and brothers couldn't get in!" said a ragged young woman cradling a feverish baby in her arms. "They gave up and went home two hours ago!"

His own mother and brothers? Andrew was confused. Was *this* the man he expected to help his father?

"That *was* strange," commented a white-whiskered man in a blue and white robe. "He just said, 'Who are My mother and My brothers?' Then He pointed to the people sitting around Him and said, 'Look! *Here* are My mother and My brothers. For whoever does the will of My Father in heaven, this one is My brother and sister and mother.' "

Father in heaven?

A ripple of wonder ran through the crowd. Something was happening inside the house. Andrew just *had* to see what it was. He pushed and shoved his way through the press of onlookers at the door, getting kicked and elbowed several times in the process. After two or three attempts, he finally succeeded in sticking his head into a narrow space between the doorpost and an elderly woman's bony shoulder.

It took a few moments for his eyes to adjust to the dim light. At first he saw nothing but lamp smoke and clouds of dust swirling in the shafts of sunlight that slanted in through the two tiny windows. Then the heads of people came into view. Next, he saw a man in a peasant's cloak and tunic, seated in their midst, raising an arm to shield himself from a shower of debris that fell from somewhere above. Then a third beam of light opened into the room. In its brightness Andrew saw a woven reed mat coming down through the ceiling. On the mat lay a man.

Suddenly a round-bellied tax collector in a Roman toga pushed in front of him, blocking his view. *Not now!* thought Andrew.

"What's happening?" shouted an old man on the left.

"He just said, 'Your sins are forgiven!' " said a rather large woman down in front. "Imagine that!"

"*Fpphh!*" spluttered the man in the blue and white robe, waving a hand in the air. "Who can forgive sins but God alone?"

But inside the house the surge of murmurs and whispers had grown to a chorus of astonished shouts. *What is it?* wondered Andrew. *I can't see a thing! If only—*

"Make way!" came a voice from within. "Let him out!"

Andrew gasped for breath. From where he stood, trapped between the tax collector, the bony woman, and the doorjamb, he could just see someone go prancing out the door. In astonishment he realized who it was—the man who had been lowered into the room on the reed mat just moments before! He had his bedroll tucked up under his arm, and he was leaping and dancing and singing.

"Praise to Yahweh!" sighed the young mother. "Jesus has healed him!"

Jesus!

"The lame walk and the blind see!" shouted someone else.

"It's the coming of the kingdom!" cried another.

The bony old woman fainted.

Then it was as if Andrew's entire world had been turned upside down. Faces, arms, and hands crossed his field of vision in a confusing blur. He was pushed and pulled from all sides at once. The crowd flowed out the door after the dancing paralytic, and Andrew was carried along in a river of oiled, perfumed, and sweating bodies. Through the flagstone courtyard it swept him, toward a jumble of stone water jars that stood beside the gate. Someone's foot caught between his legs; a large hand jammed itself against his throat and shoved him aside. He choked, then fell, striking his head against one of the jars.

When he awoke, he was lying beside the lake. It was late afternoon. Waterbirds circled and screamed overhead. Nearby sat the fishermen who had led him to the little house, mending their nets. As his head cleared, Andrew heard a voice, strong and vibrant, speaking above the murmur of waves, wind, and muffled crowd noises. He could not understand the words, but the very tone of that voice stirred something within him. He sat up and looked around.

"Ah!" said one of the fishermen. "Our young adventurer has come to his senses!"

"Lucky for him!" said another, snapping a piece of cord between his teeth.

Andrew rubbed the back of his head. There was a big lump just behind his left ear. "Ooh!" He sucked the air in between his teeth. "Where am I?"

"Lakeside," said the first fisherman. "Didn't know

where else to take you. Thought you could rest here a while. Where are your mother and father?"

Ignoring the question, Andrew turned and gazed out toward the water. There in the prow of a fishing boat anchored just offshore sat the man in the peasant tunic and cloak—Jesus. He was speaking to a crowd of people on the beach.

"What's He saying?" Andrew asked eagerly, getting to his knees and rubbing the back of his head.

"Take it easy, young master," said the fisherman, laying a callused hand on his shoulder. "You've had a nasty fall. You ought to go home."

"But I want to hear it!"

"It's just a story. I've heard it before—about a father and a son."

"A father and son? What about them?"

"Well, the son leaves home, you see," the big man began slowly, turning back to his nets. "Then, when he comes back, the father runs up to him and gives him a big hug. After that there's a family reunion and they all live happily ever after. You know, that sort of thing."

Andrew jumped to his feet. "I've got to hear this," he said. "I need to talk to Jesus!"

"Wait!" called the fisherman. But Andrew was already running as hard as he could in the direction of the crowd.

He wasn't halfway there before the gathering began

to break up. People were getting to their feet, picking up their things, and going home. Andrew slowed, stopped, and stood there rubbing the bump behind his ear, a dizzy feeling in his head. The story was over! He was too late!

To make things worse, Jesus and the other men in the boat were casting off and putting out into the lake. *Leaving!* Already they were rowing away and raising their sail.

The sun was sliding into the far west.

Andrew stared at the ship as it moved away from him. He *had* to get to Jesus. He hesitated. His mother and Aunt Hadassah would be looking for him everywhere, he knew. They would be terribly worried. They would probably get very angry. But there were worse things than that.

Down by the water's edge lay his boat—his own tight-seamed little *dancing ship*. He cast a backward glance up the beach to the town of Capernaum, its whitewashed walls and buildings turning bronze in the fading light. He pictured the crowded house, the shouting people, the paralyzed man as he went leaping out the door.

Then, without another thought, he ran down to his boat, pushed it out into the water, leaped aboard, and began rowing for all he was worth.

Alone on the lake in his *dancing ship*, Andrew pursued the man called Jesus. Stroke after stroke, labored breath by labored breath, he poured his heart and soul into the chase. *I've got to catch Him*, he thought. *For Father. It's his only chance!*

Soon a stiff breeze began to blow. Andrew paid no attention but bent to the oars with even greater determination. Pull, lift, push, dip; pull . . . Glancing over his shoulder, he saw Jesus' boat about half a stade ahead, running swiftly before the wind, its triangular sail bellied out beyond the curve of its pointed prow.

I'll never make it at this rate, he thought. *I've got to go faster somehow!* Even as he watched, the distance between the big fishing boat and his own small craft widened.

Andrew shipped one of his oars. Then, using the other to hold the boat steady, he slipped the sheet rope from its cleat, hauled the slanting yardarm to the masthead, and unfurled the small sail. With a snap, the triangle of canvas caught the wind. The little boat bounced forward.

No sooner had he raised the sail than the wind increased in strength, whipping Andrew's brown hair, gray cloak, and white tunic around his face and head. *Good,* he thought, steering straight for the fishing boat. He could almost see the faces of the men as their vessel rose and fell over the watery ridges and dipped into the troughs between the choppy waves.

Suddenly something plopped on the back of his head. It was a raindrop.

He turned. Another struck him on the cheek. Then another. To the northeast, all was dark as night. Black clouds, seamed with gray-green threads, were bunching up straight over his head, rapidly blocking out the fading light of the summer evening sky. *A storm!* Andrew felt his stomach tighten. *Strike the sail!* he thought, reaching for the sheet rope. But before he could get a firm grip on it, the wind gusted violently, throwing him into the bottom of the boat. There was a loud *crack!* and a *snap!* as the mast splintered and the little sail burst.

Frantically, his heart pounding, he refitted his oars into the oarlocks and took two strokes. All at once, the nose of the boat plunged under an oncoming wave. The stern flipped up, catapulting Andrew forward and slamming him against the curved prow. Lightning flashed. Thunder ripped through the air. A driving, pelting rain lashed the tiny boat. Breathing hard, fighting dizziness, Andrew desperately scrambled back to the bench and seized the oars again.

For a moment he sat without moving. His head spun. His arms felt wooden. Caught in one of Kinneret's unpredictable storms! The scene in the cave and the words of his father came back to him: "Alone? . . . No. Absolutely not. Not without Stephen or Demas or me."

Something—a flash of anger as bright as the lightning—exploded within him. He shouted and screamed and lashed the raging foam with his oars. The boat tipped to one side, then the other. Andrew leaned back and peered over the tops of the seething waves. Jesus and His boat were nowhere in sight.

"One day there came a storm," he heard his mother saying. "Benjamin was out on the lake alone in a small boat, like this one. He never came back."

Pictures filled his mind. His mother's face. His father taking her in his arms, kissing her on the forehead, stroking her long, brown hair. Lyra and old Baal coming in at the courtyard gate. All four of them sitting down to a dinner of flat bread and steaming broth.

"Mother!" cried Andrew, turning his face up into the pouring rain. "Father! Baal! Zeus! Meonen! Somebody! Anybody! Help me!"

At that instant a wave that seemed the size of a small mountain rammed the boat from the left side. There was a splintering sound. In a rush and tumble of foam and spray and water, Andrew and his *dancing ship* were overturned and thrust beneath the surface of the water.

And then there was darkness—darkness and bubbles and a ceaseless churning motion, up and down, side to side, as Andrew held his breath for what seemed like an eternity. He wondered what it would be like to drown, to feel the cold water gushing into his lungs, filling him like a stone jar, cutting off his life and breath, driving him to the bottom of the lake.

Then, just as he felt that his lungs would burst, his head broke the surface. Coughing, spluttering, and sobbing, he flailed around with his arms until his right hand touched something solid. It was one of the cedar planks from the shell of his boat. He seized it and held it tightly to his chest, clinging to it for his very life. It was smooth, finely shaped, expertly crafted.

Jesus. Even in the midst of the wind and rain and surging blackness, that name forced its way to the top of his consciousness. He opened his mouth, shouting at the sky, "Jesus!" At that moment, another wave crashed over him, filling his mouth with water and pushing him below the surface again.

Spinning and turning in a dark and watery abyss, Andrew fought the urge to gasp for air. Images of sea monsters flashed before his eyes. Leviathan. Rahab. Gigantic, scaly, serpentine bodies, backs ribbed with razor-sharp spines. *I'm going to die*, he thought. Within his own mind, he offered up one last desperate prayer: *Jesus! Help me!*

A surge pushed him upward, combined with a rush of sound. Then silence. And, oddly enough, moonlight. He looked around. His head was above the surface. He was breathing freely, gripping his plank, floating on water as smooth as glass. Overhead, the clouds were parting, revealing a spattering of stars and a pale white moon. *Is this the land of the dead?* he wondered. *Sheol? Or Hades?*

But it wasn't. It was Galilee under a clearing sky on a summer evening. It was Lake Kinneret, as calm and serene as he had ever seen it. It was almost as if the violent storm had been a dream. *Where did it go?* he wondered.

He turned around. There, gleaming silver in the light of the moon, its image reflected in the surface of the water as in a mirror, loomed the rocky bulk of the cliffs on the lake's southern shore. The Haunts of the Dead. The place of his father's mad wanderings. The road home.

With his last ounce of strength, Andrew paddled to shore and dragged himself onto the pebbly beach. There he sat down and put his head in his hands, feeling as if he were in a dream. He had been sitting there for what seemed a very long time, gratefully gulping down the sweet night air, when he was startled by a familiar sound—the sound of calm waters slapping the smooth sides of a wooden vessel.

He lifted his eyes. There, just offshore, stood the big fishing boat, its polished prow and white sail shining in the moonlight. And from the boat, first through the shallow water, then over the pebbles and sand of the narrow beach, strode a man.

Jesus.

This must *be a dream!* thought Andrew. Jesus was coming! And with Him were several other men—fishermen, like the ones who had befriended Andrew in Capernaum. It was too good to be true.

Jesus the healer had come! Jesus would cure his father. At last Jacob would be himself again. Their troubles would be over. Everything would be the way it used to be!

Shakily, Andrew got to his feet. He opened his mouth to shout to the man on the shore. And then—

"*Aaaaiiiieeeeeeee!*"

His call was cut short by a bloodcurdling cry. He turned to see a fearsome shape—half animal, half human—come hurtling down the path from the cliff and onto the beach. His father.

Once on level ground, the shape picked up speed. There could be no mistake about where he was headed. Like an arrow shot from a sturdy bow, he flew over the sand straight toward Jesus, screaming and gesturing wildly all the way.

The scene among the tombs thrust itself into Andrew's mind. He remembered the frantic cries and wails of old Anath and Enkidu. He thought of the two poor travelers, beaten and bloodied on their way to Gadara. In despair, he dropped to his knees and covered his face.

He'll kill him! he thought. *Father will kill Jesus!*

Kneeling there with his face in his hands, Andrew found himself wishing he'd been drowned in the storm. *Now I'll never get my father back*, he thought. *He'll kill Jesus! And then Artemas will have Father put to death!* Jesus had been his last hope, and now hope was gone. In silence he waited for the inevitable.

Then he heard a voice. "What do I have to do with You, Jesus? You Son of the Most High God! Have You come to torment us before the time?"

Such a strange voice! Rasping, ragged-edged, utterly foreign and inhuman—a voice, it seemed, made up of many voices, all of them tortured and strained. Andrew raised his head at the dreadful sound.

He was not prepared for the sight that greeted his eyes. The men who had followed Jesus up the beach were running back to their boat. But their leader stood straight and still upon the sand, His face calm, His hands at His sides, His dark hair ruffled in the early morning breeze.

His gaze was directed downward at a figure on the ground.

Father?

Was it possible? *Could that horrible voice be coming from my father?* wondered Andrew.

There was no mistaking Jacob's physical appearance. He was naked, bruised, and bleeding. His wrists and ankles bore the marks of the iron fetters. Writhing and foaming at the mouth, he lay on his face in the sand at Jesus' feet, like a tormented but submissive dog. It was a picture that filled Andrew with feelings of fear, awe, and pity.

When they were ankle-deep in the water, the fishermen stopped and turned. Some of them stood fingering the knives and swords that hung from their belts. Again Andrew found himself holding his breath.

Then Jesus spoke. "What," He said, "is your name?"

"Legion!" screamed the voices that burst from his father's mouth. "Legion is my name! For we are many!"

Andrew froze. *Legion!* Another picture flashed before his mind's eye—thousands of Roman soldiers, terrible with their flashing shields and spears, marching through Gadara's northwest gate.

Now he'll kill Him for sure! Andrew thought. *And me, too!*

Andrew jumped up and looked around for a way of escape. The night had passed; a dim glow, full of the promise of day, pulsed in the east. To the south, at the top of the cliff, a small clump of observers stood gaping down at the scene on the shore. Even at this distance, Andrew knew who they were—Demas and the other pig boys.

Even here, even now, he thought absently. *Even when I'm about to die, Demas can't leave me alone.*

"The swine! The pigs!" Jacob was on his knees, trembling from head to toe, gripping Jesus' ankle with one hand and pointing up at the cliffs with the other. "Up there! Let us go into the swine!" screamed the voices. "Don't send us away into the Abyss! The pigs, not the pit!"

For a moment, Jesus stood gazing up at the plateau. Andrew saw His brow wrinkle and the edges of His bearded lips curve downward in the hint of a frown. But in the next moment His eyes dropped decisively to the man who lay groveling at His feet. Instantly, the clouded expression cleared like mist before the rising sun.

"Very well, then," He said. "Go!" Then Andrew saw the hand of Jesus—a strong, work-hardened hand like his father's—reach down and touch a lock of Jacob's dirt-encrusted, twig-matted hair.

A pause. Then Jacob convulsed violently, cried out, and fell to the ground. Silence.

What now? Andrew took one hesitant step toward

Jesus and his father. He was about to take another when—

Rrrmmrrbbbbllmbl!

Thunder! Another storm! But from the south? Storms on Lake Kinneret almost always came down out of the north. Pivoting on his heel, Andrew looked up at the cliffs.

What he saw nearly took his breath away. There, amid clouds of rising dust or smoke (he didn't know which), a dark torrent suddenly poured over the edge of the plateau, obscuring the rocks and cave tombs. Was it a flood? Andrew stared hard. He could not tell.

The ground beneath his feet trembled as the torrent fell farther and drew nearer. Now he could see that it was not made up of water at all but of solid shapes—stones or boulders, perhaps.

An avalanche! He turned to run. But then a new sound reached his ears—a sound made up of squeals, grunts, screams, and the shouts of angry herdsmen. He squinted up at the cliff again. All at once he realized what he was seeing.

Pigs. Hundreds of them. Rushing headlong down the crags and onto the sandy beach. On and on they thundered, past the boat shed, past Andrew and Jacob and Jesus, past the astonished fishermen, straight into the lake—splashing, floundering, drowning. In a matter of moments there was nothing left of them but bubbles and foam on the surface of the waves. Andrew could do nothing but stare.

He was shaken out of his reverie by the sound of a comfortingly familiar voice calling to him from the lake. "Andrew!"

Looking out beyond the spot where the pigs had plunged into the water, he saw a boat approaching. And in the boat two familiar faces—his mother and Uncle Yohanan!

"Thank heaven you're safe!" called Helena.

Uncle Yohanan leaned on his oars and wiped his brow.

Then came another well-known voice, behind him this time. "Well! A man never knows *what* he'll find when he comes to work!"

"Stephen!" shouted Andrew in surprise. "Lyra!"

"And old Baal, too!" piped up Lyra. As always, the gray goat was pulling a small cart with a worn rag doll aboard.

Together, Stephen and Andrew ran down to the water's edge to help Helena out of the boat.

"Helena," said Stephen. "I didn't expect you back until—"

Andrew interrupted him. "Mother, I—"

Helena hugged her son, then held him at arm's length. She looked at him severely. "What were you thinking, Andrew? When we saw that your boat was gone, we realized what must have happened. We followed you as soon as the storm ended . . . so suddenly and strangely."

"A miracle—that's what it was," said old Uncle Yohanan, climbing ashore and tossing his oars into the boat. Then he sat down and mopped his forehead again.

Suddenly Andrew's mother raised her hand in a silencing gesture. "Look!" she said, her eyes as round as two silver coins.

They followed her gaze up the beach. There, at the feet of Jesus, in the middle of a circle of 10 or 12 men, sat Jacob, wrapped snugly in a brown fisherman's cloak. Gratitude, relief, and intelligence shone from his weary face.

"Jacob!" screamed Helena. Her hand shot to her mouth. Her face went white. Then she picked up her skirts and rushed toward her husband, who was already on his feet and running to meet her.

Andrew glanced over at Stephen. Stephen grinned back. "Well," he said with a shrug, "I guess that's that!"

Andrew was about to give Stephen a good-natured punch in the arm when out of the corner of his eye he saw his father coming toward him—running, just like the father in the story the fishermen had heard Jesus tell.

What now? He backed away, trembling. Should he run? Would his father attack him, attempt to strike him as he had done in the cave? Was this only a dream after all? Or was Jacob really cured, really himself again? Andrew's face burned. He started to shake. He felt cold perspiration break out on his forehead.

And then, before he had time to think another thought, he found himself enfolded in his father's strong arms, his face against his father's chest, weeping hot tears into the brown folds of the fisherman's cloak.

CHAPTER 13

It was about the third hour of the day, and all of them—Father, Mother, Andrew, Lyra, Uncle Yohanan, Stephen, and Jesus and His men—were sitting together, roasting a breakfast of carp and catfish over the glowing coals of a wood fire.

Andrew sat looking out over the sun-flecked waters of the lake. Distantly, he recalled the cold, the darkness, and the hopelessness he had known while struggling beneath their surface the night before. A feeling of unreality flooded over him. His father restored! Normal! Somehow or other, he couldn't believe it, didn't trust it. Somehow he felt he must stay on his guard.

"See! Old Baal likes it too," said Lyra, letting the goat gobble a piece of fish out of her open palm.

"Is there anything old Baal doesn't like?" scoffed Andrew.

Lyra ignored him. "And look what else he can do," she added, jumping up. Without introduction or explanation, she led the goat, cart and all, straight up to Jesus.

Oh, no! thought Andrew. *She's going to embarrass us all! She's going to ruin everything!* He got to his feet, feeling that Lyra had to be stopped before she did something to shatter this fragile, beautiful dream. Old Baal? A goat named after a pagan god? What would Jesus think? He wouldn't understand. He might even get angry. He might change His mind about Father.

But the silent man in the peasant cloak and tunic showed no sign of anger. Instead, He looked down at the little girl and her goat, smiling as she drew near. Lyra smiled back. Then, as Andrew stood rooted to the ground, wondering whether to grab her arm and yank her back, she took the rag doll from the little wooden cart and held it out to Jesus with both hands.

"For You," she said. "From old Baal—and from me, too. For helping my daddy. Her name is Iphigenia."

Andrew's jaw tensed as he waited for Jesus' response. But Jesus said nothing. Instead, His smile broadened and He bent to brush a strand of stray hair away from Lyra's nose. Then He took the little rag baby from her hands and gently tucked it into His belt.

Andrew breathed a sigh of relief. But in the next moment he heard the sound of approaching voices and footsteps. He spun around and saw 20 or 30 men and boys heading straight toward the little group gathered around the fire. Some were carrying sticks and clubs. At the head of the group strode Demas, jabbering and pointing a stubby finger at Jesus. Beside him stumped his portly uncle, his face as round and red as a juicy ham.

Demas! If Lyra can't spoil everything, Demas will!

"A word with you, sir," called Artemas. "With *all* of you." The rotund figure waddled into the circle and stepped straight up to Jesus. A few of the fishermen scrambled to their feet and drew their weapons.

"There is the little matter of my herd!" whined the pig farmer. With every word, his voice rose in pitch. "Extremely valuable animals, I assure You. Destroyed this very morning!"

"Yeah! And *he* did it!" volunteered Demas, pointing at Jesus. "With some kind of *Jew* magic! I saw it myself! From up on the cliffs!"

"Payment of some kind is in order!" demanded Artemas. "What do you plan to give me in exchange for my property?"

There was a pause. Andrew's fists tightened involuntarily.

"What about a man's life?" said Stephen quietly.

Artemas stared. "What man's life? What are you talking about?"

"*My* life, Artemas," said Jacob. In silent amazement Andrew watched his father rise slowly to his feet. There was a light in Jacob's eyes. Andrew realized in a moment that he was a different man than he had been. It was a realization that frightened him even more than the insane things his father had done while possessed by demons.

As for Artemas, he was dumbfounded. It was the first time Andrew had ever seen the man speechless. His mouth dropped open. His face looked like a slab of bacon—half red, half white. Anyone would have thought that his eyes were about to pop out of their sockets. "You!" he squealed at last. "I might have known *you* had something to do with this! But . . . how? How is it possible?"

"I can tell you that," said Andrew, stepping to the center of the circle. "Demas is right. This man," he said, pointing to Jesus, *"healed* my father! I watched Him do it!"

There was a murmur from the crowd.

"But it wasn't magic!" Andrew went on. "It was . . . well, something else. It was—" he flushed, faltered, and groped for words. "It was the work of the one true God! Jesus saved my father when nobody else could! And that's worth all the pigs in the world, if you ask me!"

An odd silence fell upon the gathering. Artemas stood shifting his gaze from Jesus to Jacob and back to Jesus again.

"So," he said at last, "the game is clear to me now. My nephew was right! It's a case of Jews, Jews, and more Jews! Jews with their tricks! Jews with their infernal rules against eating pig flesh! Jews bent on destroying my business, determined to undermine my trade! Am I right? Am I right?"

"No, Artemas!" Andrew heard his father say.

"What next?" continued Artemas. "Does every single Jew in Galilee intend to relocate to our side of the lake?"

Andrew glanced over at Jesus, wishing, hoping, and praying that He might do something to silence the pig man. But Jesus said nothing. He sat perfectly still, His sad eyes fixed on Artemas's face.

"Go on! Get out of here!" The pig farmer had worked himself into a frenzy. "Get back on your boat! Go back to your Jew towns! We don't want you around here!"

By this time the crowd was shouting with him. Jesus' friends raised their blades, ready to strike in defense of their Master. But Jesus simply stood up, turned without a word, and walked down to the big fishing boat. The fishermen hesitated a moment, then they followed Him.

"You sure told them, Uncle!" said Demas, grinning stupidly.

Artemas smirked and mopped his dripping brow with a silk handkerchief.

"Too bad, *Bar Meshugga!*" added Demas with a sneer as the crowd broke up and moved off. "Looks like you lose again!"

Andrew was too tired to respond. Exhausted and

shaken, he sank down beside Lyra and his mother. *I guess that's that*, he thought.

That was when he caught sight of his father.

Jacob stood unmoving, eyes fixed, jaw set, watching Jesus and His friends climb aboard their high-prowed fishing boat. Suddenly he stooped and kissed his wife's forehead. "Helena," Andrew heard him say as he took her by the hand, "I'm sorry—I don't know how to tell you this—but . . ."

The blood was pounding in Andrew's temples. He didn't know what his father was about to say, but he felt certain it was something he would rather not hear.

"Everything is different now," Jacob went on. "*I'm* different. And somehow . . . well, I can't help feeling that my place is with *Him*."

Tears stood in his mother's eyes. Andrew saw them glinting in the morning light. She nodded as if she understood, but she said nothing. Andrew wanted to scream, but he was powerless to utter a sound. Instead, he stood paralyzed, rooted to the ground. Helpless, he watched as his mother released her husband's hand.

With that, Jacob turned and followed Jesus down to the water's edge.

CHAPTER 14

So. It was just as he had suspected. His father—taken away from him *again*. As quickly and as unexpectedly as he had been restored. And by the very man who had healed him!

Jesus, he thought, *how can You do this to me?*

Andrew couldn't stand to watch his father climb aboard that boat. To see him sail away, across the lake, out of his life and his mother's and sister's lives—for good. Tears clouded his vision. *It's the way things always go*, he thought. *Benjamin was taken away from my father; now my father's being taken away from me!*

Anger as hot as the rising summer sun steamed inside him. All his thoughts were fogged and blurred. He bit his lower lip and clenched his fists. Then he turned and ran to the path at the base of the cliff, to the trail that wound among the rocks and tombs.

To the Haunts of the Dead.

"Why?" shouted Andrew to the echoing caverns.

"Why did you give him back, only to take him away again?"

Finding the open tomb that had once sheltered him and his father from the storm, he fell inside and pressed his cheek against the cold stone floor. *The one true God!* he thought bitterly.

True God, false gods—what was the difference? Either way, an 11-year-old boy didn't stand a chance. He sat up, seized a rock, and hurled it with all his might toward the lake. It fell with a harmless rustle in a hyssop bush about 50 feet down the cliff.

Yes, the gods were angry at him. Hadn't the villagers known it all along? Wasn't this why Artemas wanted to keep the Jews from coming to Gadara? The Jews would not acknowledge the power of Zeus, Sin, Baal, and lucky Meonen. The Jews had funny customs and strange beliefs of their own. And he, Andrew, had delivered his own father into the hands of a Jew! He pounded his fist against the rock until it bled.

At last his supply of hot tears was spent. He could cry no more. Drained, empty, and oddly quiet inside, Andrew sat up and looked out the door of the cave. Far out on the lake he could see the big fishing boat moving off toward the north—to Capernaum.

Capernaum.

Unbidden, pictures of the day he had spent in the town on the north shore flooded back into his mind. The small white house, bursting with people. The glittering motes of dust in the beam of light that broke through the hole in the ceiling. The paralyzed man, his mat rolled up under his arm, dancing out the courtyard gate. The smile on the face of Jesus as He brushed twigs and bits of clay from His hair and beard.

Jesus. For weeks that name had possessed his imagination. He had called upon that name in the midst of the churning waves. At that name the waves and wind had become calm, suddenly and strangely calm.

And now Andrew could hear the voice of Jesus again—calming, soothing, stirring, challenging. He saw the face of Jesus—frowning up at the cliffs, smiling down at his little sister and her pet goat. And the hands of Jesus—touching his father's matted hair, sending the evil spirits into the herd of pigs, tucking the rag doll into His belt.

Could the hands of any god heal more powerfully than those hands? *No*, he thought. And wouldn't a god's face—if there were any god worth fearing or loving in heaven above or the earth below—look like that face? Wouldn't any god worthy of the name have a voice like the voice of Jesus? Wouldn't he say the kinds of things that Jesus said? *Yes*, thought Andrew. *It would have to be so.*

In that moment the words of Jesus came back to him: "Who are My mother and My brothers? . . . Whoever does the will of My Father in heaven, this one is My brother and sister and mother."

Gazing out at the boat as it raised its sail and faded into the blue of the lake, Andrew thought hard about those words. The picture that had loomed before him in the face of death leaped before his mind's eye again: a leather mat spread on the paving stones of the courtyard; great round disks of hot bread and wooden bowls filled with steaming broth; Lyra sneaking her vegetables to old Baal when Mother wasn't looking; Father urging Andrew to have more broth.

Father. "The will of My Father in heaven." Never before had Andrew heard of any god called "Father"— *Abba*, Daddy. What if it were true? And what if that Father-God really wanted Andrew's father to follow Jesus? What if that were His will, after all? Could any father be more powerful, more loving than *that* Father? Did any family matter more than *His* family? Perhaps, thought Andrew, just perhaps, Jesus needed Jacob more than Andrew and his mother and Lyra did. And what could be better than knowing that his father was working for Jesus?

Andrew jumped up. "What have I been thinking?" he shouted, fixing his eyes on the distant speck that he knew to be the fishing boat. "Who am *I* to keep my father from doing the will of *his* Father?"

He fell to the floor once again and squeezed his eyes

shut. "Jesus," he whispered into the darkness of the cave, "if You really want my father, You can have him! He belongs to You now. After all, *You* made him well!"

He heard footsteps on the path outside. A hand touched him on the shoulder. He looked up to see his mother's face.

"Your father thought we might find you here," she said softly.

"H-he did?" stammered Andrew.

It was true. There at her side stood Jacob. And bunched up behind him were the beaming faces of Lyra, Stephen, and the scraggly-bearded goat.

The sun was high in the sky now. Its light streamed in at the cavern door. Jacob reached down, took Andrew by the hand, and drew him to his feet.

"Come on, son," he said. "Let's go home."

t was late in the afternoon. Coppery sunlight was slanting across the waves and splashing up against the
smooth trunks of the palms around the lake.

Ssshh-k! Ssshh-k! Ssshh-k!

Andrew stopped planing, wiped his dripping forehead, and looked up at his father, who stood just outside
the shed, deep in conversation with the grizzled old merchant captain. "It was what *He* wanted," Jacob was saying. "I would have followed that man anywhere. Anywhere! But He wouldn't let me. Ordered me to go back
home, back to my family—to the people of Gadara—to
tell everyone what He'd done for me. As if I could keep
my mouth shut!"

"Good for Him," drawled the captain. "We need you
here, Jacob. Anybody with the power to give you back
to us, whether god or man . . . well, I'm on *His* side,
that's all." He paused to spit in the sand. "As for those
pigs," he added, raising an eyebrow and lowering his
voice, "good riddance to 'em! You should've had a whiff

of my hold after I hauled that one load up to Gergesa. Phew-*eee!*" The two men broke into loud guffaws. Andrew leaned against the workbench and grinned. It was good to hear his father laugh again.

"Whatcha doin'?" said Lyra, running up, jumping through the air, and landing on her knees in the sand. The old gray goat trudged along after her, stopping every so often to chew stray tufts of beach grass. In the little cart behind him rode a brand-new doll—a wooden doll. Andrew smiled, remembering what fun it had been to watch his father carve it, sitting with him under the billowing awning outside the door to their house on a warm summer evening.

"I'm building a new boat," proclaimed Andrew in answer to his sister's question. "Father's helping me this time, so it's going to be even better than the first one. I've learned from my mistakes."

"That's good!" said Lyra. Then, as if remembering something far more important than Andrew and his boat, she jumped up, tossed her hair over her shoulder, and trotted off to join a group of children who were playing along the shore.

"Off to a great start," said Stephen, ducking in under the awning and giving Andrew a wink. "Think you'll be doing any *solo* trips in this one?"

Andrew grinned. "No. I don't think I'll ever do *anything* alone again!"

"Everything's ready!" It was his mother calling. She stood a short distance up the beach, between the boat shed and the shining cliffs, spreading a leather tarp on the sand beside a small wood fire and setting out reed baskets of bread and fish. "Supper on the beach tonight!"

"Hurray!" shouted Andrew, dropping his tools on the workbench and running to help Helena with the picnic. "Come on, Lyra! Supper on the beach!"

But Lyra couldn't hear him. She was too busy dancing and singing with the other boys and girls on the shore. Andrew could hear their song drifting up from the water's edge, mingling with the evening cries of the birds and the music of the lapping waves:

> Jacob and Jesus down by the shore,
> Jacob's not crazy anymore!

"Andrew," said Helena, filling a wooden bowl with grapes and pomegranates and glancing up at the men, "your father seems a little . . . preoccupied. Do you think you could convince him to join us for supper?"

Andrew picked up a loaf of the hot bread, sniffed it, and smiled. "*That* shouldn't take a miracle!" he said.

Letters From Our Readers

I know I've seen this story in the Bible before. But I can't find it.

Callum M., Dallas, TX

The basis for this story is found in the New Testament of the Bible: Mark 4:35–5:20 and Luke 8:22–39. In both the calming of the storm and in the casting out of the demons from the man, the power God gave Jesus is evident.

You won't find any mention of Andrew in the biblical accounts. We have imagined what it must have been like for the family of this man possessed by demons. Surely he had people who loved him and were concerned about him. Imagine their joy when he was healed. There must have been lots of hugs and laughter that day.

Notice that the events in this story take place right before the story about Jairus' daughter, a story we tell in *The Worst Wish*, another KidWitness Tales book.

Did Jesus really have a doll that a little girl gave Him?

Brittany N., Las Vegas, Nevada

That is not in the Bible. But we presume many people gave Jesus gifts from their hearts that the Bible does not record. We feel if Jesus did get a doll, He would thank the giver and value that doll because He loved the one who gave it to Him. We also know Jesus loved children.

Why isn't the lake called the Sea of Galilee?

Angie I., Fresno, OH

The Sea of Galilee (which isn't really a sea at all, but a freshwater lake) was known by several different names in Jesus' time. Galilee was one of them; the others were Kinneret or Chinneroth (which comes from a Hebrew word meaning "harp"—after the shape of the lake), Gennesaret, and Tiberias. We chose Kinneret because it is the oldest name of the lake (going back to Old Testament times) and for that reason was probably the most common with the Jewish people in those days.

Why is this book so scary?

Bridget E., Boise, Idaho

Anytime someone becomes involved with demons, things get very scary because the power of evil is frightening. Demons are not harmless as television and movies might tell us. Although demons and spirits can seem to be friendly and to possess knowledge and power we want to have, getting involved with them is always disastrous.

However, there is good news! If you belong to Jesus there is no need to be afraid. For if you belong to Jesus, you cannot belong to anyone else. Not only that, but also it is good to know that God is bigger, stronger, and more powerful than evil. There is a verse that says, "Greater is He who is in you than he who is in the world" (1 John 4:4, NASB). God has more power than any demon or so-called god (see *Trouble Times Ten*, another KidWitness book). With your hand in His, you never need to be afraid. When I'm afraid I like to read Psalm 91. It reminds me that no matter what happens, God is always with me. —ed.

What was happening to Crazy Jacob? Why was he going crazy?

Megan W., Bangor, Maine

Since Jacob believed in whatever "god" might help him, he opened up his heart to some evil spirits. He didn't put his trust in God, but in many other things. He wasn't really "crazy" but was allowing himself to be controlled by demons. The more the demons took over, the more strange and destructive his behavior became. Only God was more powerful than the demons. And since Jesus is God, He could send the demons away.

Are all "crazy" people just demon-possessed?

Megan J., Venice, Florida

No. There are many illnesses which affect the normal functions of our brains. Our brains are very fragile. It doesn't take much to damage them. That's why we try hard to protect them by wearing helmets when we ride bikes, or being careful what foods we eat or medicines we take. Our brains are a great gift from God! We need to take good care of them.